Lyrics of Lowly Life

Lyrics of
Lowly Life
Paul Laurence Dunbar

MINT EDITIONS

Lyrics of Lowly Life was first published in 1897.

This edition published by Mint Editions 2021.

ISBN 9781513295428 | E-ISBN 9781513295572

Published by Mint Editions®

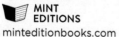 MINT
EDITIONS

minteditionbooks.com

Publishing Director: Jennifer Newens
Design & Production: Rachel Lopez Metzger
Project Manager: Micaela Clark
Typesetting: Westchester Publishing Services

Contents

Ere Sleep Comes Down to Soothe
the Weary Eyes

Ere sleep comes down to soothe the weary eyes,
Which all the day with ceaseless care have sought
The magic gold which from the seeker flies;
Ere dreams put on the gown and cap of thought,
And make the waking world a world of lies,—
Of lies most palpable, uncouth, forlorn,
That say life's full of aches and tears and sighs,—
Oh, how with more than dreams the soul is torn,
Ere sleep comes down to soothe the weary eyes.

Ere sleep comes down to soothe the weary eyes,
How all the griefs and heartaches we have known
Come up like pois'nous vapors that arise
From some base witch's caldron, when the crone
To work some potent spell, her magic plies.
The past which held its share of bitter pain,
Whose ghost we prayed that Time might exorcise,
Comes up, is lived and suffered o'er again,
Ere sleep comes down to soothe the weary eyes.

Ere sleep comes down to soothe the weary eyes,
What phantoms fill the dimly lighted room;
What ghostly shades in awe-creating guise
Are bodied forth within the teeming gloom.
What echoes faint of sad and soul-sick cries,
And pangs of vague inexplicable pain
That pay the spirit's ceaseless enterprise,
Come thronging through the chambers of the brain,
Ere sleep comes down to soothe the weary eyes.

Ere sleep comes down to soothe the weary eyes,
Where ranges forth the spirit far and free?
Through what strange realms and unfamiliar skies
Tends her far course to lands of mystery?
To lands unspeakable—beyond surmise,

Where shapes unknowable to being spring,
Till, faint of wing, the Fancy fails and dies
Much wearied with the spirit's journeying,
Ere sleep comes down to soothe the weary eyes.

Ere sleep comes down to soothe the weary eyes,
How questioneth the soul that other soul,—
The inner sense which neither cheats nor lies,
But self exposes unto self, a scroll
Full writ with all life's acts unwise or wise,
In characters indelible and known;
So, trembling with the shock of sad surprise,
The soul doth view its awful self alone,
Ere sleep comes down to soothe the weary eyes.

When sleep comes down to seal the weary eyes,
The last dear sleep whose soft embrace is balm,
And whom sad sorrow teaches us to prize
For kissing all our passions into calm,
Ah, then, no more we heed the sad world's cries,
Or seek to probe th' eternal mystery,
Or fret our souls at long-withheld replies,
At glooms through which our visions cannot see,
When sleep comes down to seal the weary eyes.

The Poet and His Song

A Song is but a little thing,
And yet what joy it is to sing!
In hours of toil it gives me zest,
And when at eve I long for rest;
When cows come home along the bars,
And in the fold I hear the bell,
As Night, the shepherd, herds his stars,
I sing my song, and all is well.

There are no ears to hear my lays,
No lips to lift a word of praise;
But still, with faith unfaltering,
I live and laugh and love and sing.
What matters yon unheeding throng?
They cannot feel my spirit's spell,
Since life is sweet and love is long,
I sing my song, and all is well.

My days are never days of ease;
I till my ground and prune my trees.
When ripened gold is all the plain,
I put my sickle to the grain.
I labor hard, and toil and sweat,
While others dream within the dell;
But even while my brow is wet,
I sing my song, and all is well.

Sometimes the sun, unkindly hot,
My garden makes a desert spot;
Sometimes a blight upon the tree
Takes all my fruit away from me;
And then with throes of bitter pain
Rebellious passions rise and swell;
But—life is more than fruit or grain,
And so I sing, and all is well.

Retort

"Thou art a fool," said my head to my heart,
"Indeed, the greatest of fools thou art,
To be led astray by the trick of a tress,
By a smiling face or a ribbon smart;"
And my heart was in sore distress.

Then Phyllis came by, and her face was fair,
The light gleamed soft on her raven hair;
And her lips were blooming a rosy red.
Then my heart spoke out with a right bold air:
"Thou art worse than a fool, O head!"

Accountability

Folks ain't got no right to censuah othah folks about dey habits;
Him dat giv' de squir'ls de bushtails made de bobtails fu' de rabbits.
Him dat built de gread big mountains hollered out de little valleys,
Him dat made de streets an' driveways wasn't shamed to make de
    alleys.

We is all constructed diff'ent, d'ain't no two of us de same;
We cain't he'p ouah likes an' dislikes, ef we 'se bad we ain't to blame.
If we 'se good, we needn't show off, case you bet it ain't ouah doin'
We gits into su'ttain channels dat we jes' cain't he'p pu'suin'.

But we all fits into places dat no othah ones could fill,
And we does the things we has to, big er little, good er ill.
John cain't tek de place o' Henry, Su an' Sally ain't alike;
Bass ain't nuthin' like a suckah, chub ain't nuthin' like a pike.

When you come to think about it, how it 's all planned out it 's
    splendid.
Nuthin's done er evah happens, 'dout hit's somefin' dat's intended;
Don't keer what you does, you has to, an' hit sholy beats de dickens,—
Viney, go put on de kittle, I got one o' mastah's chickens.

Frederick Douglass

A Hush is over all the teeming lists,
And there is pause, a breath-space in the strife;
A spirit brave has passed beyond the mists
And vapors that obscure the sun of life.
And Ethiopia, with bosom torn,
Laments the passing of her noblest born.

She weeps for him a mother's burning tears—
She loved him with a mother's deepest love.
He was her champion thro' direful years,
And held her weal all other ends above.

When Bondage held her bleeding in the dust,
He raised her up and whispered, "Hope and Trust."

For her his voice, a fearless clarion, rung
That broke in warning on the ears of men;
For her the strong bow of his power he strung,
And sent his arrows to the very den
Where grim Oppression held his bloody place
And gloated o'er the mis'ries of a race.

And he was no soft-tongued apologist;
He spoke straightforward, fearlessly uncowed;
The sunlight of his truth dispelled the mist,
And set in bold relief each dark-hued cloud;
To sin and crime he gave their proper hue,
And hurled at evil what was evil's due.

Through good and ill report he cleaved his way
Right onward, with his face set toward the heights,
Nor feared to face the foeman's dread array,—
The lash of scorn, the sting of petty spites.
He dared the lightning in the lightning's track,
And answered thunder with his thunder back.

When men maligned him, and their torrent wrath
In furious imprecations o'er him broke,
He kept his counsel as he kept his path;
'Twas for his race, not for himself, he spoke.
He knew the import of his Master's call,
And felt himself too mighty to be small.

No miser in the good he held was he,—
His kindness followed his horizon's rim.
His heart, his talents, and his hands were free
To all who truly needed aught of him.
Where poverty and ignorance were rife,
He gave his bounty as he gave his life.

The place and cause that first aroused his might
Still proved its power until his latest day.
In Freedom's lists and for the aid of Right
Still in the foremost rank he waged the fray;
Wrong lived; his occupation was not gone.
He died in action with his armor on!

We weep for him, but we have touched his hand,
And felt the magic of his presence nigh,
The current that he sent throughout the land,
The kindling spirit of his battle-cry.
O'er all that holds us we shall triumph yet,
And place our banner where his hopes were set!

Oh, Douglass, thou hast passed beyond the shore,
But still thy voice is ringing o'er the gale!
Thou'st taught thy race how high her hopes may soar,
And bade her seek the heights, nor faint, nor fail.
She will not fail, she heeds thy stirring cry,
She knows thy guardian spirit will be nigh,
And, rising from beneath the chast'ning rod,
She stretches out her bleeding hands to God!

LIFE

A Crust of bread and a corner to sleep in,
A minute to smile and an hour to weep in,
A pint of joy to a peck of trouble,
And never a laugh but the moans come double;
And that is life!

A crust and a corner that love makes precious,
With the smile to warm and the tears to refresh us;
And joy seems sweeter when cares come after,
And a moan is the finest of foils for laughter;
And that is life!

The Lesson

My cot was down by a cypress grove,
And I sat by my window the whole night long,
And heard well up from the deep dark wood
A mocking-bird's passionate song.

And I thought of myself so sad and lone,
And my life's cold winter that knew no spring;
Of my mind so weary and sick and wild,
Of my heart too sad to sing.

But e'en as I listened the mock-bird's song,
A thought stole into my saddened heart,
And I said, "I can cheer some other soul
By a carol's simple art."

For oft from the darkness of hearts and lives
Come songs that brim with joy and light,
As out of the gloom of the cypress grove
The mocking-bird sings at night.

So I sang a lay for a brother's ear
In a strain to soothe his bleeding heart,
And he smiled at the sound of my voice and lyre,
Though mine was a feeble art.

But at his smile I smiled in turn,
And into my soul there came a ray:
In trying to soothe another's woes
Mine own had passed away.

The Rising of the Storm

The lake's dark breast
Is all unrest,
It heaves with a sob and a sigh.
Like a tremulous bird,
From its slumber stirred,
The moon is a-tilt in the sky.

From the silent deep
The waters sweep,
But faint on the cold white stones,
And the wavelets fly
With a plaintive cry
O'er the old earth's bare, bleak bones.

And the spray upsprings
On its ghost-white wings,
And tosses a kiss at the stars;
While a water-sprite,
In sea-pearls dight,
Hums a sea-hymn's solemn bars.

Far out in the night,
On the wavering sight
I see a dark hull loom;
And its light on high,
Like a Cyclops' eye,
Shines out through the mist and gloom.

Now the winds well up
From the earth's deep cup,
And fall on the sea and shore,
And against the pier
The waters rear
And break with a sullen roar.

PAUL LAURENCE DUNBAR

Up comes the gale,
And the mist-wrought veil
Gives way to the lightning's glare,
And the cloud-drifts fall,
A sombre pall,
O'er water, earth, and air.

The storm-king flies,
His whip he plies,
And bellows down the wind.
The lightning rash
With blinding flash
Comes pricking on behind.

Rise, waters, rise,
And taunt the skies
With your swift-flitting form.
Sweep, wild winds, sweep,
And tear the deep
To atoms in the storm.

And the waters leapt,
And the wild winds swept,
And blew out the moon in the sky,
And I laughed with glee,
It was joy to me
As the storm went raging by!

Sunset

The river sleeps beneath the sky,
And clasps the shadows to its breast;
The crescent moon shines dim on high;
And in the lately radiant west
The gold is fading into gray.
Now stills the lark his festive lay,
And mourns with me the dying day.

While in the south the first faint star
Lifts to the night its silver face,
And twinkles to the moon afar
Across the heaven's graying space,
Low murmurs reach me from the town,
As Day puts on her sombre crown,
And shakes her mantle darkly down.

THE OLD APPLE-TREE

There's a memory keeps a-runnin'
Through my weary head tonight,
An' I see a picture dancin'
In the fire-flames' ruddy-light;
'Tis the picture of an orchard
Wrapped in autumn's purple haze,
With the tender light about it
That I loved in other days.
An' a-standin' in a corner
Once again I seem to see
The verdant leaves an' branches
Of an old apple-tree.

You perhaps would call it ugly,
An' I don't know but it's so,
When you look the tree all over
Unadorned by memory's glow;
For its boughs are gnarled an' crooked,
An' its leaves are gettin' thin,
An' the apples of its bearin'
Wouldn't fill so large a bin
As they used to. But I tell you,
When it comes to pleasin' me,
It's the dearest in the orchard,—
Is that old apple-tree.

I would hide within its shelter,
Settlin' in some cosy nook,
Where no calls nor threats could stir me
From the pages o' my book.
Oh, that quiet, sweet seclusion
In its fulness passeth words!
It was deeper than the deepest
That my sanctum now affords.
Why, the jaybirds an' the robins,

They was hand in glove with me,
As they winked at me 'an warbled
In that old apple-tree.

It was on its sturdy branches
That in summers long ago
I would tie my swing an' dangle
In contentment to an' fro,
Idly dreaming' childish fancies,
Buildin' castles in the air,
Makin' o' myself a hero
Of romances rich an' rare.
I kin shet my eyes an' see it
Jest as plain as plain kin be,
That same old swing a-danglin'
To the old apple-tree.

There's a rustic seat beneath it
That I never kin forget.
It's the place where me an' Hallie—
Little sweetheart—used to set,
When we'd wander to the orchard
So's no listenin' ones could hear
As I whispered sugared nonsense
Into her little willin' ear.
Now my gray old wife is Hallie,
An' I'm grayer still than she,
But I'll not forget our courtin'
'Neath the old apple-tree,

Life for us ain't all been summer,
But I guess we've had our share
Of its flittin' joys an' pleasures,
An' a sprinklin' of its care.
Oft the skies have smiled upon us;
Then again we've seen 'em frown,
Though our load was ne'er so heavy
That we longed to lay it down.

But when death does come a-callin',
This my last request shall be,—
That they'll bury me an' Hallie
'Neath the old apple-tree.

A Prayer

O Lord, the hard-won miles
Have worn my stumbling feet:
Oh, soothe me with thy smiles,
And make my life complete.

The thorns were thick and keen
Where'er I trembling trod;
The way was long between
My wounded feet and God.

Where healing waters flow
Do thou my footsteps lead.
My heart is aching so;
Thy gracious balm I need.

Passion and Love

A Maiden wept and, as a comforter,
Came one who cried, "I love thee," and he seized
Her in his arms and kissed her with hot breath,
That dried the tears upon her flaming cheeks.
While evermore his boldly blazing eye
Burned into hers; but she uncomforted
Shrank from his arms and only wept the more.

Then one came and gazed mutely in her face
With wide and wistful eyes; but still aloof
He held himself; as with a reverent fear,
As one who knows some sacred presence nigh.
And as she wept he mingled tear with tear,
That cheered her soul like dew a dusty flower,—
Until she smiled, approached, and touched his hand!

The Seedling

As a quiet little seedling
Lay within its darksome bed,
To itself it fell a-talking,
And this is what it said:

"I am not so very robust,
But I'll do the best I can;"
And the seedling from that moment
Its work of life began.

So it pushed a little leaflet
Up into the light of day,
To examine the surroundings
And show the rest the way.

The leaflet liked the prospect,
So it called its brother, Stem;
Then two other leaflets heard it,
And quickly followed them.

To be sure, the haste and hurry
Made the seedling sweat and pant;
But almost before it knew it
It found itself a plant.

The sunshine poured upon it,
And the clouds they gave a shower;
And the little plant kept growing
Till it found itself a flower.

Little folks, be like the seedling,
Always do the best you can;
Every child must share life's labor
Just as well as every man.

And the sun and showers will help you
Through the lonesome, struggling hours,
Till you raise to light and beauty
Virtue's fair, unfading flowers.

PROMISE

I Grew a rose within a garden fair,
And, tending it with more than loving care,
I thought how, with the glory of its bloom,
I should the darkness of my life illume;
And, watching, ever smiled to see the lusty bud
Drink freely in the summer sun to tinct its blood.

My rose began to open, and its hue
Was sweet to me as to it sun and dew;
I watched it taking on its ruddy flame
Until the day of perfect blooming came,
Then hasted I with smiles to find it blushing red—
Too late! Some thoughtless child had plucked my rose and fled!

Fulfilment

I Grew a rose once more to please mine eyes.
All things to aid it—dew, sun, wind, fair skies—
Were kindly; and to shield it from despoil,
I fenced it safely in with grateful toil.
No other hand than mine shall pluck this flower, said I,
And I was jealous of the bee that hovered nigh.

It grew for days; I stood hour after hour
To watch the slow unfolding of the flower,
And then I did not leave its side at all,
Lest some mischance my flower should befall.
At last, oh joy! the central petals burst apart.
It blossomed—but, alas! a worm was at its heart!

Song

My heart to thy heart,
My hand to thine;
My lips to thy lips,
Kisses are wine
Brewed for the lover in sunshine and shade;
Let me drink deep, then, my African maid.

Lily to lily,
Rose unto rose;
My love to thy love
Tenderly grows.
Rend not the oak and the ivy in twain,
Nor the swart maid from her swarthier swain.

An Ante-Bellum Sermon

We is gathahed hyeah, my brothahs,
In dis howlin' wildaness,
Fu' to speak some words of comfo't
To each othah in distress.
An' we chooses fu' ouah subjic'
Dis—we'll 'splain it by an' by;
"An' de Lawd said, 'Moses, Moses,'
An' de man said, 'Hyeah am I.'"

Now ole Pher'oh, down in Egypt,
Was de wuss man evah bo'n,
An' he had de Hebrew chillun
Down dah wukin' in his co'n;
'T well de Lawd got tiahed o' his foolin',
An' sez he: "I'll let him know—
Look hyeah, Moses, go tell Pher'oh
Fu' to let dem chillun go."

"An' ef he refuse to do it,
I will make him rue de houah,
Fu' I'll empty down on Egypt
All de vials of my powah."
Yes, he did—an' Pher'oh's ahmy
Wasn't wuth a ha'f a dime;
Fu' de Lawd will he'p his chillun,
You kin trust him evah time.

An' yo' enemies may 'sail you
In de back an' in de front;
But de Lawd is all aroun' you,
Fu' to ba' de battle's brunt.
Dey kin fo'ge yo' chains an' shackles
F'om de mountains to de sea;
But de Lawd will sen' some Moses
Fu' to set his chillun free.

An' de lan' shall hyeah his thundah,
Lak a blas' f'om Gab'el's ho'n,
Fu' de Lawd of hosts is mighty
When he girds his ahmor on.
But fu' feah some one mistakes me,
I will pause right hyeah to say,
Dat I'm still a-preachin' ancient,
I ain't talkin' 'bout today.

But I tell you, fellah christuns,
Things'll happen mighty strange;
Now, de Lawd done dis fu' Isrul,
An' his ways don't nevah change,
An, de love he showed to Isrul
Wasn't all on Isrul spent;
Now don't run an' tell yo' mastahs
Dat I's preachin' discontent.

'Cause I isn't; I'se a-judgin'
Bible people by deir ac's;
I'se a-givin' you de Scriptuah,
I'se a-handin' you de fac's.
Cose ole Pher'oh b'lieved in slav'ry,
But de Lawd he let him see,
Dat de people he put bref in,—
Evah mothah's son was free.

An' dahs othahs thinks lak Pher'oh,
But dey calls de Scriptuah liar,
Fu' de Bible says "a servant
Is a-worthy of his hire."
An' you cain't git roun' nor thoo dat
An' you cain't git ovah it,
Fu' whatevah place you git in,
Dis hyeah Bible too 'll fit.

So you see de Lawd's intention,
Evah sence de worl' began,
Was dat His almighty freedom

Should belong to evah man,
But I think it would be bettah,
Ef I'd pause agin to say,
Dat I'm talkin' 'bout ouah freedom
In a Bibleistic way.

But de Moses is a-comin',
An' he's comin', suah and fas'
We kin hyeah his feet a-trompin',
We kin hyeah his trumpit blas'.
But I want to wa'n you people,
Don't you git too brigity;
An' don't you git to braggin'
'Bout dese things, you wait an' see.

But when Moses wif his powah
Comes an' sets us chillun free,
We will praise de gracious Mastah
Dat has gin us liberty;
An' we'll shout ouah halleluyahs,
On dat mighty reck'nin' day,
When we'se reco'nised ez citiz'
Huh uh! Chillun, let us pray!

Ode to Ethiopia

O Mother Race! to thee I bring
This pledge of faith unwavering,
This tribute to thy glory.
I know the pangs which thou didst feel,
When Slavery crushed thee with its heel,
With thy dear blood all gory.

Sad days were those—ah, sad indeed!
But through the land the fruitful seed
Of better times was growing.
The plant of freedom upward sprung,
And spread its leaves so fresh and young—
Its blossoms now are blowing.

On every hand in this fair land,
proud Ethiope's swarthy children stand
Beside their fairer neighbor;
The forests flee before their stroke,
Their hammers ring, their forges smoke,
They stir in honest labour.

They tread the fields where honour calls;
Their voices sound through senate halls
In majesty and power.
To right they cling; the hymns they sing
Up to the skies in beauty ring,
And bolder grow each hour.

Be proud, my Race, in mind and soul;
Thy name is writ on Glory's scroll
In characters of fire.
High 'mid the clouds of Fame's bright sky
Thy banner's blazoned folds now fly,
And truth shall lift them higher.

PAUL LAURENCE DUNBAR

Thou hast the right to noble pride,
Whose spotless robes were purified
By blood's severe baptism.
Upon thy brow the cross was laid,
And labour's painful sweat-beads made
A consecrating chrism.

No other race, or white or black,
When bound as thou wert, to the rack,
So seldom stooped to grieving;
No other race, when free again,
Forgot the past and proved them men
So noble in forgiving.

Go on and up! Our souls and eyes
Shall follow thy continuous rise;
Our ears shall list thy story
From bards who from thy root shall spring,
And proudly tune their lyres to sing
Of Ethiopia's glory.

The Corn-Stalk Fiddle

When the corn's all cut and the bright stalks shine
Like the burnished spears of a field of gold;
When the field-mice rich on the nubbins dine,
And the frost comes white and the wind blows cold;
Then it's heigh-ho! fellows and hi-diddle-diddle,
For the time is ripe for the corn-stalk fiddle.

And when you take a stalk that is straight and long,
With an expert eye to its worthy points,
And you think of the bubbling strains of song
That are bound between its pithy joints—
Then you cut out strings, with a bridge in the middle,
With a corn-stalk bow for a corn-stalk fiddle.

Then the strains that grow as you draw the bow
O'er the yielding strings with a practiced hand!
And the music's flow never loud but low
Is the concert note of a fairy band.
Oh, your dainty songs are a misty riddle
To the simple sweets of a corn-stalk fiddle.

When the eve comes on, and our work is done,
And the sun drops down with a tender glance,
With their hearts all prime for the harmless fun,
Come the neighbor girls for the evening's dance,
And they wait for the well-known twist and twiddle—
More time than tune—from the corn-stalk fiddle.

Then brother Jabez takes the bow,
While Ned stands off with Susan Bland,
Then Henry stops by Milly Snow,
And John takes Nellie Jones's hand,
While I pair off with Mandy Biddle,
And scrape, scrape, scrape goes the corn-stalk fiddle.

"Salute your partners," comes the call,
"All join hands and circle round,"
"Grand train back," and "Balance all,"
Footsteps lightly spurn the ground.
"Take your lady and balance down the middle"
To the merry strains of the corn-stalk fiddle.

So the night goes on and the dance is o'er,
And the merry girls are homeward gone,
But I see it all in my sleep once more,
And I dream till the very break of dawn
Of an impish dance on a red-hot griddle
To the screech and scrape of a corn-stalk fiddle.

THE MASTER-PLAYER

An old worn harp that had been played
Till all its strings were loose and frayed,
Joy, Hate and Fear, each one essayed,
To play. But each in turn had found
No sweet responsiveness of sound.
Then Love the Master-Player came
With heaving breast and eyes aflame;
The harp he took all undismayed,
Smote on its strings, still strange to song,
And brought forth music sweet and strong.

The Mystery

I was not; now I am—a few days hence
I shall not be; I fain would look before
And after, but can neither do; some Power
Or lack of power says "no" to all I would.
I stand upon a wide and sunless plain,
Nor chart nor steel to guide my steps aright.
Whene'er, o'ercoming fear, I dare to move,
I grope without direction and by chance.
Some feign to hear a voice and feel a hand
That draws them ever upward thro' the gloom.
But I—I hear no voice and touch no hand,
Tho' oft thro' silence infinite I list,
And strain my hearing to supernal sounds;
Tho' oft thro' fateful darkness do I reach,
And stretch my hand to find that other hand.
I question of th' eternal bending skies
That seem to neighbor with the novice earth;
But they roll on, and daily shut their eyes
On me, as I one day shall do on them,
And tell me not the secret that I ask.

Not they Who Soar

Not they who soar, but they who plod
Their rugged way, unhelped, to God
Are heroes; they who higher fare,
And, flying, fan the upper air,
Miss all the toil that hugs the sod.
'Tis they whose backs have felt the rod,
Whose feet have pressed the path unshod,
May smile upon defeated care,
Not they who soar.
High up there are no thorns to prod,
Nor boulders lurking 'neath the clod
To turn the keenness of the share,
For flight is ever free and rare;
But heroes they the soil who've trod,
Not they who soar!

WHITTIER

Not o'er thy dust let there be spent
The gush of maudlin sentiment;
Such drift as that is not for thee,
Whose life and deeds and songs agree,
Sublime in their simplicity.

Nor shall the sorrowing tear be shed.
O singer sweet, thou art not dead!
In spite of time's malignant chill,
With living fire thy songs shall thrill,
And men shall say, "He liveth still!"

Great poets never die, for Earth
Doth count their lives of too great worth
To lose them from her treasured store;
So shalt thou live for evermore—
Though far thy form from mortal ken—
Deep in the hearts and minds of men.

Two Songs

A Bee that was searching for sweets one day
Through the gate of a rose garden happened to stray.
In the heart of a rose he hid away,
And forgot in his bliss the light of day,
As sipping his honey he buzzed in song;
Though day was waning, he lingered long,
For the rose was sweet, so sweet.

A robin sits pluming his ruddy breast,
And a madrigal sings to his love in her nest:
"Oh, the skies they are blue, the fields are green,
And the birds in your nest will soon be seen!"
She hangs on his words with a thrill of love,
And chirps to him as he sits above,
For the song is sweet, so sweet.

A maiden was out on a summer's day
With the winds and the waves and the flowers at play;
And she met with a youth of gentle air,
With the light of the sunshine on his hair.
Together they wandered the flowers among;
They loved, and loving they lingered long,
For to love is sweet, so sweet.

Bird of my lady's bower,
Sing her a song;
Tell her that every hour,
All the day long,
Thoughts of her come to me,
Filling my brain
With the warm ecstasy
Of love's refrain.

Little bird! happy bird!
Being so near,
Where e'en her slightest word

Thou mayest hear,
Seeing her glancing eyes,
Sheen of her hair,
Thou art in paradise,—
Would I were there.

I am so far away,
Thou art so near;
Plead with her, birdling gay,
Plead with my dear.
Rich be thy recompense,
Fine be thy fee,
If through thine eloquence
She hearken me.

A Banjo Song

Oh, dere's lots o' keer an' trouble
In dis world to swaller down;
An' ol' Sorrer's purty lively
In her way o' gittin' roun'.
Yet dere's times when I furgit 'em,—
Aches an' pains an' troubles all,—
An' it's when I tek at ebenin'
My ol' banjo f'om de wall.

'Bout de time dat night is fallin'
An' my daily wu'k is done,
An' above de shady hilltops
I kin see de settin' sun;
When de quiet, restful shadders
Is beginnin' jes' to fall,—
Den I take de little banjo
F'om its place upon de wall.

Den my fam'ly gadders roun' me
In de fadin' o' de light,
Ez I strike de strings to try 'em
Ef dey all is tuned er-right.
An' it seems we're so nigh heaben
We kin hyeah de angels sing
When de music o' dat banjo
Sets my cabin all er-ring.

An' my wife an' all de othahs,—
Male an' female, small an' big,—
Even up to gray-haired granny,
Seem jes' boun' to do a jig;
'Twell I change de style o' music,
Change de movement an' de time,
An' de ringin' little banjo
Plays an ol' hea't-feelin' hime.

An' somehow my th'oat gits choky,
An' a lump keeps tryin' to rise
Lak it wan'ed to ketch de water
Dat was flowin' to my eyes;
An' I feel dat I could sorter
Knock de socks clean off o' sin
Ez I hyeah my po' ol' granny
Wif huh tremblin' voice jine in.

Den we all th'ow in our voices
Fu' to he'p de chune out too,
Lak a big camp-meetin' choiry
Tryin' to sing a mou'nah th'oo.
An' our th'oahts let out de music,
Sweet an' solemn, loud an' free,
'Twell de raftahs o' my cabin
Echo wif de melody.

Oh, de music o' de banjo,
Quick an' deb'lish, solemn, slow,
Is de greates' joy an' solace
Dat a weary slave kin know!
So jes' let me hyeah it ringin',
Dough de chune be po' an' rough,
It's a pleasure; an' de pleasures
O' dis life is few enough.

Now, de blessed little angels
Up in heaben, we are told,
Don't do nothin' all dere lifetime
'Ceptin' play on ha'ps o' gold.
Now I think heaben'd be mo' homelike
Ef we'd hyeah some music fall
F'om a real ol'-fashioned banjo,
Like dat one upon de wall.

Longing

If you could sit with me beside the sea today,
And whisper with me sweetest dreamings o'er and o'er;
I think I should not find the clouds so dim and gray,
And not so loud the waves complaining at the shore.

If you could sit with me upon the shore today,
And hold my hand in yours as in the days of old,
I think I should not mind the chill baptismal spray,
Nor find my hand and heart and all the world so cold.

If you could walk with me upon the strand today,
And tell me that my longing love had won your own,
I think all my sad thoughts would then be put away,
And I could give back laughter for the Ocean's moan!

The Path

There are no beaten paths to Glory's height,
There are no rules to compass greatness known;
Each for himself must cleave a path alone,
And press his own way forward in the fight.
Smooth is the way to ease and calm delight,
And soft the road Sloth chooseth for her own;
But he who craves the flower of life full-blown,
Must struggle up in all his armor dight!
What though the burden bear him sorely down
And crush to dust the mountain of his pride,
Oh, then, with strong heart let him still abide;
For rugged is the roadway to renown,
Nor may he hope to gain the envied crown
Till he hath thrust the looming rocks aside.

The Lawyers' Way

I've been list'nin' to them lawyers
In the court house up the street,
An' I've come to the conclusion
That I'm most completely beat.
Fust one feller riz to argy,
An' he boldly waded in
As he dressed the tremblin' pris'ner
In a coat o' deep-dyed sin.

Why, he painted him all over
In a hue o' blackest crime,
An' he smeared his reputation
With the thickest kind o' grime,
Tell I found myself a-wond'rin',
In a misty way and dim,
How the Lord had come to fashion
Sich an awful man as him.

Then the other lawyer started,
An', with brimmin', tearful eyes,
Said his client was a martyr
That was brought to sacrifice.
An' he give to that same pris'ner
Every blessed human grace,
Tell I saw the light o' virtue
Fairly shinin' from his face.

Then I own 'at I was puzzled
How sich things could rightly be;
An' this aggervatin' question
Seems to keep a-puzzlin' me.
So, will some one please inform me,
An' this mystery unroll—
How an angel an' a devil
Can persess the self-same soul?

Ode for Memorial Day

Done are the toils and the wearisome marches,
Done is the summons of bugle and drum.
Softly and sweetly the sky overarches,
Shelt'ring a land where Rebellion is dumb.
Dark were the days of the country's derangement,
Sad were the hours when the conflict was on,
But through the gloom of fraternal estrangement
God sent his light, and we welcome the dawn.
O'er the expanse of our mighty dominions,
Sweeping away to the uttermost parts,
Peace, the wide-flying, on untiring pinions,
Bringeth her message of joy to our hearts.

Ah, but this joy which our minds cannot measure,
What did it cost for our fathers to gain!
Bought at the price of the heart's dearest treasure,
Born out of travail and sorrow and pain;
Born in the battle where fleet Death was flying,
Slaying with sabre-stroke bloody and fell;
Born where the heroes and martyrs were dying,
Torn by the fury of bullet and shell.
Ah, but the day is past: silent the rattle,
And the confusion that followed the fight.
Peace to the heroes who died in the battle,
Martyrs to truth and the crowning of Right!

Out of the blood of a conflict fraternal,
Out of the dust and the dimness of death,
Burst into blossoms of glory eternal
Flowers that sweeten the world with their breath.
Flowers of charity, peace, and devotion
Bloom in the hearts that are empty of strife;
Love that is boundless and broad as the ocean
Leaps into beauty and fulness of life.
So, with the singing of pæans and chorals,

And with the flag flashing high in the sun,
Place on the graves of our heroes the laurels
Which their unfaltering valor has won!

Premonition

Dear heart, good-night!
Nay, list awhile that sweet voice singing
When the world is all so bright,
And the sound of song sets the heart a-ringing,
Oh, love, it is not right—
Not then to say, "Good-night."

Dear heart, good-night!
The late winds in the lake weeds shiver,
And the spray flies cold and white.
And the voice that sings gives a telltale quiver—
"Ah, yes, the world is bright,
But, dearest heart, good-night!"

Dear heart, good-night!
And do not longer seek to hold me!
For my soul is in affright
As the fearful glooms in their pall enfold me.
See him who sang how white
And still; so, dear, good-night.

Dear heart, good-night!
Thy hand I'll press no more forever,
And mine eyes shall lose the light;
For the great white wraith by the winding river
Shall check my steps with might.
So, dear, good-night, good-night!

Retrospection

When you and I were young, the days
Were filled with scent of pink and rose,
And full of joy from dawn till close,
From morning's mist till evening's haze.
And when the robin sung his song
The verdant woodland ways along,
We whistled louder than he sung.
And school was joy, and work was sport
For which the hours were all too short,
When you and I were young, my boy,
When you and I were young.

When you and I were young, the woods
Brimmed bravely o'er with every joy
To charm the happy-hearted boy.
The quail turned out her timid broods;
The prickly copse, a hostess fine,
Held high black cups of harmless wine;
And low the laden grape-vine swung
With beads of night-kissed amethyst
Where buzzing lovers held their tryst,

When you and I were young, my boy,
When you and I were young.
When you and I were young, the cool
And fresh wind fanned our fevered brows
When tumbling o'er the scented mows,
Or stripping by the dimpling pool,
Sedge-fringed about its shimmering face,
Save where we'd worn an ent'ring place.
How with our shouts the calm banks rung!
How flashed the spray as we plunged in,—
Pure gems that never caused a sin!
When you and I were young, my boy,
When you and I were young.

When you and I were young, we heard
All sounds of Nature with delight,—
The whirr of wing in sudden flight,
The chirping of the baby-bird.
The columbine's red bells were rung;
The locust's vested chorus sung;
While every wind his zithern strung
To high and holy-sounding keys,
And played sonatas in the trees—
When you and I were young, my boy,
When you and I were young.

When you and I were young, we knew
To shout and laugh, to work and play,
And night was partner to the day
In all our joys. So swift time flew
On silent wings that, ere we wist,
The fleeting years had fled unmissed;
And from our hearts this cry was wrung—
To fill with fond regret and tears
The days of our remaining years—
"When you and I were young, my boy,
When you and I were young."

Unexpressed

Deep in my heart that aches with the repression,
And strives with plenitude of bitter pain,
There lives a thought that clamors for expression,
And spends its undelivered force in vain.

What boots it that some other may have thought it?
The right of thoughts' expression is divine;
The price of pain I pay for it has bought it,
I care not who lays claim to it—'t is mine!

And yet not mine until it be delivered;
The manner of its birth shall prove the test.
Alas, alas, my rock of pride is shivered—
I beat my brow—the thought still unexpressed.

Song of Summer

Dis is gospel weathah sho'—
Hills is sawt o' hazy.
Meddahs level ez a flo'
Callin' to de lazy.
Sky all white wif streaks o' blue,
Sunshine softly gleamin',
D'ain't no wuk hit's right to do,
Nothin' 's right but dreamin'.

Dreamin' by de rivah side
Wif de watahs glist'nin',
Feelin' good an' satisfied
Ez you lay a-list'nin'
To the little nakid boys
Splashin' in de watah,
Hollerin' fu' to spress deir joys
Jes' lak youngsters ought to.
Squir'l a-tippin' on his toes,
So's to hide an' view you;
Whole flocks o' camp-meetin' crows
Shoutin' hallelujah.
Peckahwood erpon de tree
Tappin' lak a hammah;
Jaybird chattin' wif a bee,
Tryin' to teach him grammah.

Breeze is blowin' wif perfume,
Jes' enough to tease you;
Hollyhocks is all in bloom,
Smellin' fu' to please you.
Go 'way, folks, an' let me 'lone,
Times is gettin' dearah—
Summah's settin' on de th'one,
An' I'm a-layin' neah huh!

Spring Song

A Blue-Bell springs upon the ledge,
A lark sits singing in the hedge;
Sweet perfumes scent the balmy air,
And life is brimming everywhere.
What lark and breeze and bluebird sing,
Is Spring, Spring, Spring!

No more the air is sharp and cold;
The planter wends across the wold,
And, glad, beneath the shining sky
We wander forth, my love and I.
And ever in our hearts doth ring
This song of Spring, Spring!

For life is life and love is love,
'Twixt maid and man or dove and dove.
Life may be short, life may be long,
But love will come, and to its song
Shall this refrain for ever cling
Of Spring, Spring, Spring!

PAUL LAURENCE DUNBAR

To Louise

Oh, the poets may sing of their Lady Irenes,
And may rave in their rhymes about wonderful queens;
But I throw my poetical wings to the breeze,
And soar in a song to my Lady Louise.
A sweet little maid, who is dearer, I ween,
Than any fair duchess, or even a queen.
When speaking of her I can't plod in my prose,
For she's the wee lassie who gave me a rose.

Since poets, from seeing a lady's lip curled,
Have written fair verse that has sweetened the world;
Why, then, should not I give the space of an hour
To making a song in return for a flower?
I have found in my life—it has not been so long—
There are too few of flowers—too little of song.
So out of that blossom, this lay of mine grows,
For the dear little lady who gave me the rose.

I thank God for innocence, dearer than Art,
That lights on a by-way which leads to the heart,
And led by an impulse no less than divine,
Walks into the temple and sits at the shrine.
I would rather pluck daisies that grow in the wild,
Or take one simple rose from the hand of a child,
Than to breathe the rich fragrance of flowers that bide
In the gardens of luxury, passion, and pride.

I know not, my wee one, how came you to know
Which way to my heart was the right way to go;
Unless in your purity, soul-clean and dear,
God whispers his messages into your ear.
You have now had my song, let me end with a prayer
That your life may be always sweet, happy, and fair;
That your joys may be many, and absent your woes,
O dear little lady who gave me the rose!

The Rivals

'Twas three an' thirty year ago,
I When I was ruther young, you know,
I had my last an' only fight
About a gal one summer night.
'Twas me an' Zekel Johnson; Zeke
'N' me 'd be'n spattin' 'bout a week,
Each of us tryin' his best to show
That he was Liza Jones's beau.
We couldn't neither prove the thing,
Fur she was fur too sharp to fling
One over fur the other one
An' by so doin' stop the fun
That we chaps didn't have the sense
To see she got at our expense,
But that's the way a feller does,
Fur boys is fools an' allus was.
An' when they's females in the game
I reckon men's about the same.
Well, Zeke an' me went on that way
An' fussed an' quarrelled day by day;
While Liza, mindin' not the fuss,
Jest kep' a-goin' with both of us,
Tell we pore chaps, that's Zeke an' me,
Was jest plum mad with jealousy.
Well, fur a time we kep' our places,
An' only showed by frownin' faces
An' looks 'at well our meanin' boded
How full o' fight we both was loaded.
At last it come, the thing broke out,
An' this is how it come about.
One night ('t was fair, you'll all agree)
I got Eliza's company,
An' leavin' Zekel in the lurch,
Went trottin' off with her to church.
An' jest as we had took our seat
(Eliza lookin' fair an' sweet),

Why, I jest couldn't help but grin
When Zekel come a-bouncin' in
As furious as the law allows.
He'd jest be'n up to Liza's house,
To find her gone, then come to church
To have this end put to his search.
I guess I laffed that meetin' through,
An' not a mortal word I knew
Of what the preacher preached er read
Er what the choir sung er said.
Fur every time I'd turn my head
I couldn't skeercely help but see
'At Zekel had his eye on me.
An' he 'ud sort o' turn an' twist
An' grind his teeth an' shake his fist.
I laughed, fur la! the hull church seen us,
An' knowed that suthin' was between us.
Well, meetin' out, we started hum,
I sorter feelin' what would come.
We'd jest got out, when up stepped Zeke,
An' said, "Scuse me, I'd like to speak
To you a minute." "Cert," said I—
A-nudgin' Liza on the sly
An' laughin' in my sleeve with glee,
I asked her, please, to pardon me.
We walked away a step er two,
Jest to git out o' Liza's view,
An' then Zeke said, "I want to know
Ef you think you're Eliza's beau,
An' 'at I'm goin' to let her go
Hum with sich a chap as you?"
An' I said bold, "You bet I do."
Then Zekel, sneerin', said 'at he
Didn't want to hender me.
But then he 'lowed the gal was his
An' 'at he guessed he knowed his biz,
An' wasn't feared o' all my kin
With all my friends an' chums throwed in.
Some other things he mentioned there

That no born man could no ways bear
Er think o' ca'mly tryin' to stan'
Ef Zeke had be'n the bigges' man
In town, an' not the leanest runt
'At time an' labor ever stunt.
An' so I let my fist go "bim,"
I thought I'd mos' nigh finished him.
But Zekel didn't take it so.
He jest ducked down an' dodged my blow
An' then come back at me so hard,
I guess I must 'a' hurt the yard,
Er spilet the grass plot where I fell,
An' sakes alive it hurt me; well,
It wouldn't be'n so bad, you see,
But he jest kep' a-hittin' me.
An' I hit back an' kicked an' pawed,
But 't seemed 'twas mostly air I clawed,
While Zekel used his science well
A-makin' every motion tell.
He punched an' hit, why, goodness lands,
Seemed like he had a dozen hands.
Well, afterwhile they stopped the fuss,
An' some one kindly parted us.
All beat an' cuffed an' clawed an' scratched,
An' needin' both our faces patched,
Each started hum a different way;
An' what o' Liza, do you say,
Why, Liza—little humbug—dern her,
Why, she'd gone home with Hiram Turner.

The Lover and the Moon

A Lover whom duty called over the wave,
With himself communed: "Will my love be true
If left to herself? Had I better not sue
Some friend to watch over her, good and grave?
But my friend might fail in my need," he said,
"And I return to find love dead.
Since friendships fade like the flow'rs of June,
I will leave her in charge of the stable moon."

Then he said to the moon: "O dear old moon,
Who for years and years from thy throne above
Hast nurtured and guarded young lovers and love,
My heart has but come to its waiting June,
And the promise time of the budding vine;
Oh, guard thee well this love of mine."
And he harked him then while all was still,
And the pale moon answered and said, "I will."

And he sailed in his ship o'er many seas,
And he wandered wide o'er strange far strands:
in isles of the south and in Orient lands,
Where pestilence lurks in the breath of the breeze.
But his star was high, so he braved the main,
And sailed him blithely home again;
And with joy he bended his footsteps soon
To learn of his love from the matron moon.

She sat as of yore, in her olden place,
Serene as death, in her silver chair.
A white rose gleamed in her whiter hair,
And the tint of a blush was on her face.
At sight of the youth she sadly bowed
And hid her face 'neath a gracious cloud.
She faltered faint on the night's dim marge,
But "How," spoke the youth, "have you kept your charge?"

The moon was sad at a trust ill-kept;
The blush went out in her blanching cheek,
And her voice was timid and low and weak,
As she made her plea and sighed and wept.
"Oh, another prayed and another plead,
And I couldn't resist," she answering said;
"But love still grows in the hearts of men:
Go forth, dear youth, and love again."

But he turned him away from her proffered grace.
"Thou art false, O moon, as the hearts of men,
I will not, will not love again."
And he turned sheer 'round with a soul-sick face
To the sea, and cried: "Sea, curse the moon,
Who makes her vows and forgets so soon."
And the awful sea with anger stirred,
And his breast heaved hard as he lay and heard.

And ever the moon wept down in rain,
And ever her sighs rose high in wind;
But the earth and sea were deaf and blind,
And she wept and sighed her griefs in vain.
And ever at night, when the storm is fierce,
The cries of a wraith through the thunders pierce;
And the waves strain their awful hands on high
To tear the false moon from the sky.

Conscience and Remorse

"Good-Bye," I said to my conscience—
"Good-bye for aye and aye,"
And I put her hands off harshly,
And turned my face away;
And conscience smitten sorely
Returned not from that day.

But a time came when my spirit
Grew weary of its pace;
And I cried: "Come back, my conscience;
I long to see thy face."
But conscience cried: "I cannot;
Remorse sits in my place."

IONE

I

Ah, yes, 't is sweet still to remember,
Though 't were less painful to forget;
For while my heart glows like an ember,
Mine eyes with sorrow's drops are wet,
And, oh, my heart is aching yet.
It is a law of mortal pain
That old wounds, long accounted well,
Beneath the memory's potent spell,
Will wake to life and bleed again.

So 't is with me; it might be better
If I should turn no look behind,—
If I could curb my heart, and fetter
From reminiscent gaze my mind,
Or let my soul go blind—go blind!
But would I do it if I could?
Nay! ease at such a price were spurned;
For, since my love was once returned,
All that I suffer seemeth good.

I know, I know it is the fashion,
When love has left some heart distressed,
To weight the air with wordful passion;
But I am glad that in my breast
I ever held so dear a guest.
Love does not come at every nod,
Or every voice that calleth "hasten;"
He seeketh out some heart to chasten,
And whips it, wailing, up to God!

Love is no random road wayfarer
Who Where he may must sip his glass.
Love is the King, the Purple-Wearer,
Whose guard recks not of tree or grass

To blaze the way that he may pass.
What if my heart be in the blast
That heralds his triumphant way;
Shall I repine, shall I not say:
"Rejoice, my heart, the King has passed!"

In life, each heart holds some sad story—
The saddest ones are never told.
I, too, have dreamed of fame and glory,
And viewed the future bright with gold;
But that is as a tale long told.
Mine eyes have lost their youthful flash,
My cunning hand has lost its art;
I am not old, but in my heart
The ember lies beneath the ash.

I loved! Why not? My heart was youthful,
My mind was filled with healthy thought.
He doubts not whose own self is truthful,
Doubt by dishonesty is taught;
So loved! boldly, fearing naught.
I did not walk this lowly earth;
Mine was a newer, higher sphere,
Where youth was long and life was dear,
And all save love was little worth.

Her likeness! Would that I might limn it,
As Love did, with enduring art;
Nor dust of days nor death may dim it,
Where it lies graven on my heart,
Of this sad fabric of my life a part.
I would that I might paint her now
As I beheld her in that day,
Ere her first bloom had passed away,
And left the lines upon her brow.

A face serene that, beaming brightly,
Disarmed the hot sun's glances bold.
A foot that kissed the ground so lightly,

He frowned in wrath and deemed her cold,
But loved her still though he was old.
A form where every maiden grace
Bloomed to perfection's richest flower,—
The statued pose of conscious power,
Like lithe-limbed Dian's of the chase.

Beneath a brow too fair for frowning,
Like moon-lit deeps that glass the skies
Till all the hosts above seem drowning,
Looked forth her steadfast hazel eyes,
With gaze serene and purely wise.
And over all, her tresses rare,
Which, when, with his desire grown weak,
The Night bent down to kiss her cheek,
Entrapped and held him captive there.

This was Ione; a spirit finer
Ne'er burned to ash its house of clay;
A soul instinct with fire diviner
Ne'er fled athwart the face of day,
And tempted Time with earthly stay.
Her loveliness was not alone
Of face and form and tresses' hue;
For aye a pure, high soul shone through
Her every act: this was Ione.

II

'Twas in the radiant summer weather,
When God looked, smiling, from the sky;
And we went wand'ring much together
By wood and lane, Ione and I,
Attracted by the subtle tie
Of common thoughts and common tastes,
Of eyes whose vision saw the same,
And freely granted beauty's claim
Where others found but worthless wastes.

We paused to hear the far bells ringing
Across the distance, sweet and clear.
We listened to the wild bird's singing
The song he meant for his mate's ear,
And deemed our chance to do so dear.
We loved to watch the warrior Sun,
With flaming shield and flaunting crest,
Go striding down the gory West,
When Day's long fight was fought and won.

And life became a different story;
Where'er I looked, I saw new light.
Earth's self assumed a greater glory,
Mine eyes were cleared to fuller sight.
Then first I saw the need and might
Of that fair band, the singing throng,
Who, gifted with the skill divine,
Take up the threads of life, spun fine,
And weave them into soulful song.

They sung for me, whose passion pressing
My soul, found vent in song nor line.
They bore the burden of expressing
All that I felt, with art's design,
And every word of theirs was mine.
I read them to Ione, ofttimes,
By hill and shore, beneath fair skies,
And she looked deeply in mine eyes,
And knew my love spoke through their rhymes.

Her life was like the stream that floweth,
And mine was like the waiting sea;
Her love was like the flower that bloweth,
And mine was like the searching bee—
I found her sweetness all for me.
God plied him in the mint of time,
And coined for us a golden day,
And rolled it ringing down life's way
With love's sweet music in its chime.

And God unclasped the Book of Ages,
And laid it open to our sight;
Upon the dimness of its pages,
So long consigned to rayless night,
He shed the glory of his light.
We read them well, we read them long,
And ever thrilling did we see
That love ruled all humanity,—
The master passion, pure and strong.

III

Today my skies are bare and ashen,
And bend on me without a beam.
Since love is held the master-passion,
Its loss must be the pain supreme—
And grinning Fate has wrecked my dream.
But pardon, dear departed Guest,
I will not rant, I will not rail;
For good the grain must feel the flail;
There are whom love has never blessed.

I had and have a younger brother,
One whom I loved and love today
As never fond and doting mother
Adored the babe who found its way
From heavenly scenes into her day.
Oh, he was full of youth's new wine,—
A man on life's ascending slope,
Flushed with ambition, full of hope;
And every wish of his was mine.

A kingly youth; the way before him
Was thronged with victories to be won;
so joyous, too, the heavens o'er him
Were bright with an unchanging sun,—
His days with rhyme were overrun.
Toil had not taught him Nature's prose,
Tears had not dimmed his brilliant eyes,

And sorrow had not made him wise;
His life was in the budding rose.

I know not how I came to waken,
Some instinct pricked my soul to sight;
My heart by some vague thrill was shaken,—
A thrill so true and yet so slight,
I hardly deemed I read aright.
As when a sleeper, ign'rant why,
Not knowing what mysterious hand
Has called him out of slumberland,
Starts up to find some danger nigh.

Love is a guest that comes, unbidden,
But, having come, asserts his right;
He will not be repressed nor hidden.
And so my brother's dawning plight
Became uncovered to my sight.
Some sound-mote in his passing tone
Caught in the meshes of my ear;
Some little glance, a shade too dear,
Betrayed the love he bore Ione.

What could I do? He was my brother,
And young, and full of hope and trust;
I could not, dared not try to smother
His flame, and turn his heart to dust.
I knew how oft life gives a crust
To starving men who cry for bread;
But he was young, so few his days,
He had not learned the great world's ways,
Nor Disappointment's volumes read.

However fair and rich the booty,
I could not make his loss my gain.
For love is dear, but dearer, duty,
And here my way was clear and plain.
I saw how I could save him pain.
And so, with all my day grown dim,

That this loved brother's sun might shine,
I joined his suit, gave over mine,
And sought Ione, to plead for him.

I found her in an eastern bower,
Where all day long the am'rous sun
Lay by to woo a timid flower.
This day his course was well-nigh run,
But still with lingering art he spun
Gold fancies on the shadowed wall.
The vines waved soft and green above,
And there where one might tell his love,
I told my griefs—I told her all!

I told her all, and as she hearkened,
A tear-drop fell upon her dress.
With grief her flushing brow was darkened;
One sob that she could not repress
Betrayed the depths of her distress.
Upon her grief my sorrow fed,
And I was bowed with unlived years,
My heart swelled with a sea of tears,
The tears my manhood could not shed.

The world is Rome, and Fate is Nero,
Disporting in the hour of doom.
God made us men; times make the hero—
But in that awful space of gloom
I gave no thought but sorrow's room.
All—all was dim within that bower,
What time the sun divorced the day;
And all the shadows, glooming gray,
Proclaimed the sadness of the hour.

She could not speak—no word was needed;
Her look, half strength and half despair,
Told me I had not vainly pleaded,
That she would not ignore my prayer.
And so she turned and left me there,

And as she went, so passed my bliss;
She loved me, I could not mistake—
But for her own and my love's sake,
Her womanhood could rise to this!

My wounded heart fled swift to cover,
And life at times seemed very drear.
My brother proved an ardent lover—
What had so young a man to fear?
He wed Ione within the year.
No shadow clouds her tranquil brow,
Men speak her husband's name with pride,
While she sits honored at his side—
She is—she must be happy now!

I doubt the course I took no longer,
Since those I love seem satisfied.
The bond between them will grow stronger
As they go forward side by side;
Then will my pains be justified.
Their joy is mine, and that is best—
I am not totally bereft,
For I have still the mem'ry left—
Love stopped with me—a Royal Guest!

Religion

I am no priest of crooks nor creeds,
For human wants and human needs
Are more to me than prophets' deeds;
And human tears and human cares
Affect me more than human prayers.

Go, cease your wail, lugubrious saint!
You fret high Heaven with your plaint.
Is this the "Christian's joy" you paint?
Is this the Christian's boasted bliss?
Avails your faith no more than this?

Take up your arms, come out with me,
Let Heav'n alone; humanity
Needs more and Heaven less from thee.
With pity for mankind look 'round;
Help them to rise—and Heaven is found.

Deacon Jones' Grievance

I've been watchin' of 'em parson,
An' I'm sorry fur to say
'At my mind is not contented
With the loose an' keerless way
'At the young folks treat the music;
'Tain't the proper sort o' choir.
Then I don't believe in Christuns
A-singin' hymns for hire.

But I never would 'a' murmured
An' the matter might 'a' gone
Ef it wasn't fur the antics
'At I've seen 'em kerry on;
So I thought it was my dooty
Fur to come to you an' ask
Ef you wouldn't sort o' gently
Take them singin' folks to task.

Fust, the music they're be'n singin'
Will disgrace us mighty soon;
It's a cross between a opry
An' a ol' cotillion tune.
With its dashes an' its quavers
An' its hifalutin style—
Why, it sets my head to swimmin'
When I'm comin' down the aisle.

Now it might be almost decent
Ef it wasn't fur the way
'At they git up there an' sing it,
Hey dum diddle, loud and gay.
Why, it shames the name o' sacred
In its brazen worldliness,
An' they're even got "Ol' Hundred"
In a bold, new-fangled dress.

You'll excuse me, Mr. Parson,
Ef I seem a little sore;
But I've sung the songs of Isr'el
For threescore years an' more,
An' it sort o' hurts my feelin's
Fur to see 'em put away
Fur these harum-scarum ditties
'At is capturin' the day.

There's anuther little happ'nin'
'At I'll mention while I'm here,
Jes' to show 'at my objections
All is offered sound and clear.
It was one day they was singin'
An' was doin' well enough—
Singin' good as people could sing
Sich an awful mess o' stuff—

When the choir give a holler,
An' the organ give a groan,
An' they left one weak-voiced feller
A-singin' there alone!
But he stuck right to the music,
Tho' 't was tryin' as could be;
An' when I tried to help him,
Why, the hull church scowled at me.

You say that's so-low singin',
Well, I pray the Lord that I
Growed up when folks was willin'
To sing their hymns so high.
Why, we never had sich doin's
In the good ol' Bethel days,
When the folks was all contented
With the simple songs of praise.

Now I may have spoke too open,
But 't was too hard to keep still,
An' I hope you'll tell the singers

'At I bear 'em no ill-will.
'At they all may git to glory
Is my wish an' my desire,
But they'll need some extry trainin'
'Fore they jine the heavenly choir.

ALICE

Know you, winds that blow your course
Down the verdant valleys,
That somewhere you must, perforce,
Kiss the brow of Alice?
When her gentle face you find,
Kiss it softly, naughty wind.

Roses waving fair and sweet
Thro' the garden alleys,
Grow into a glory meet
For the eye of Alice;
Let the wind your offering bear
Of sweet perfume, faint and rare.
Lily holding crystal dew
In your pure white chalice,
Nature kind hath fashioned you
Like the soul of Alice;
It of purest white is wrought,
Filled with gems of crystal thought.

After the Quarrel

So we, who've supped the self-same cup,
Tonight must lay our friendship by;
Your wrath has burned your judgment up,
Hot breath has blown the ashes high.
You say that you are wronged—ah, well,
I count that friendship poor, at best
A bauble, a mere bagatelle,
That cannot stand so slight a test.

I fain would still have been your friend,
And talked and laughed and loved with you
But since it must, why, let it end;
The false but dies, 't is not the true.
So we are favored, you and I,
Who only want the living truth.
It was not good to nurse the lie;
'Tis well it died in harmless youth.

I go from you tonight to sleep.
Why, what's the odds? why should I grieve?
I have no fund of tears to weep
For happenings that undeceive.
The days shall come, the days shall go
Just as they came and went before.
The sun shall shine, the streams shall flow
Though you and I are friends no more.

And in the volume of my years,
Where all my thoughts and acts shall be,
The page whereon your name appears
Shall be forever sealed to me.
Not that I hate you over-much,
'Tis less of hate than love defied;
Howe'er, our hands no more shall touch,
We'll go our ways, the world is wide.

Beyond the Years

I

Beyond the years the answer lies,
Beyond where brood the grieving skies
And Night drops tears.
Where Faith rod-chastened smiles to rise
And doff its fears,
And carping Sorrow pines and dies—
Beyond the years.

II

Beyond the years the prayer for rest
Shall beat no more within the breast;
The darkness clears,
And Morn perched on the mountain's crest
Her form uprears—
The day that is to come is best,
Beyond the years.

III

Beyond the years the soul shall find
That endless peace for which it pined,
For light appears,
And to the eyes that still were blind
With blood and tears,
Their sight shall come all unconfined
Beyond the years.

After a Visit

I be'n down in ole Kentucky
Fur a week er two, an' say,
'Twuz ez hard ez breakin' oxen
Fur to tear myse'f away.
Allus argerin' 'bout fren'ship
An' yer hospitality—
Y' ain't no right to talk about it
Tell you be'n down there to see.

See jest how they give you welcome
To the best that's in the land,
Feel the sort o' grip they give you
When they take you by the hand.
Hear 'em say, "We're glad to have you,
Better stay a week er two;"
An' the way they treat you makes you
Feel that ev'ry word is true.

Feed you tell you hear the buttons
Crackin' on yore Sunday vest;
Haul you roun' to see the wonders
Tell you have to cry for rest.
Drink yer health an' pet an' praise you
Tell you git to feel ez great
Ez the Sheriff o' the county
Er the Gov'ner o' the State.

Wife, she sez I must be crazy
'Cause I go on so, an' Nelse
He 'lows, "Goodness gracious! daddy,
Cain't you talk about nuthin' else?"
Well, pleg-gone it, I'm jes' tickled,
Bein' tickled ain't no sin;
I be'n down in ole Kentucky,
An' I want o' go ag'in.

CURTAIN

Villain shows his indiscretion,
Villain's partner makes confession.
Juvenile, with golden tresses,
Finds her pa and dons long dresses.
Scapegrace comes home money-laden,
Hero comforts tearful maiden,
Soubrette marries loyal chappie,
Villain skips, and all are happy.

PAUL LAURENCE DUNBAR

The Spellin'-Bee

I never shall furgit that night when father hitched up Dobbin,
An' all us youngsters clambered in an' down the road went bobbin'
To school where we was kep' at work in every kind o' weather,
But where that night a spellin'-bee was callin' us together.
'Twas one o' Heaven's banner nights, the stars was all a glitter,
The moon was shinin' like the hand o' God had jest then lit her.
The ground was white with spotless snow, the blast was sort o' stingin';
But underneath our round-abouts, you bet our hearts was singin'.
That spellin'-bee had be'n the talk o' many a precious moment,
The youngsters all was wild to see jes' what the precious show meant,
An' we whose years was in their teens was little less desirous
O' gittin' to the meetin' so's our sweethearts could admire us.
So on we went so anxious fur to satisfy our mission
That father had to box our ears, to smother our ambition.
But boxin' ears was too short work to hinder our arrivin',
He jest turned roun' an' smacked us all, an' kep' right on a-drivin'.
Well, soon the schoolhouse hove in sight, the winders beamin'
    brightly;
The sound o' talkin' reached our ears, and voices laffin' lightly.
It puffed us up so full an' big 'at I'll jest bet a dollar,
There wa'n't a feller there but felt the strain upon his collar.
So down we jumped an' in we went ez sprightly ez you make 'em,
But somethin' grabbed us by the knees an' straight began to shake 'em.
Fur once within that lighted room, our feelin's took a canter,
An' scurried to the zero mark ez quick ez Tam O'Shanter.
'Cause there was crowds o' people there, both sexes an' all stations;
It looked like all the town had come an' brought all their relations.
The first I saw was Nettie Gray, I thought that girl was dearer
'N' gold; an' when I got a chance, you bet I aidged up near her.
An' Farmer Dobbs's girl was there, the one 'at Jim was sweet on,
An' Cyrus Jones an' Mandy Smith an' Faith an' Patience Deaton.
Then Parson Brown an' Lawyer Jones were present—all attention,
An' piles on piles of other folks too numerous to mention.
The master rose an' briefly said: "Good friends, dear brother Crawford,
To spur the pupils' minds along, a little prize has offered.
To him who spells the best tonight—or 't may be 'her'—no tellin'—

He offers ez a jest reward, this precious work on spellin'."
A little blue-backed spellin'-book with fancy scarlet trimmin';
We boys devoured it with our eyes—so did the girls an' women.
He held it up where all could see, then on the table set it,
An' ev'ry speller in the house felt mortal bound to get it.
At his command we fell in line, prepared to do our dooty,
Outspell the rest an' set 'em down, an' carry home the booty.
'Twas then the merry times began, the blunders, an' the laffin',
The nudges an' the nods an' winks an' stale good-natured chaffin'.
Ole Uncle Hiram Dane was there, the clostest man a-livin',
Whose only bugbear seemed to be the dreadful fear o' givin'.
His beard was long, his hair uncut, his clothes all bare an' dingy;
It wasn't 'cause the man was pore, but jest so mortal stingy.
An' there he sot by Sally Riggs a-smilin' an' a-smirkin',
An' all his childern lef' to home a diggin' an' a-workin'.
A widower he was, an' Sal was thinkin' 'at she'd wing him;
I reckon he was wond'rin' what them rings o' hern would bring him.
An' when the spellin'-test commenced, he up an' took his station,
A-spellin' with the best o' them to beat the very nation.
An' when he'd spell some youngster down, he'd turn to look at Sally,
An' say: "The teachin' nowadays can't be o' no great vally."
But true enough the adage says, "Pride walks in slipp'ry places,"
Fur soon a thing occurred that put a smile on all our faces.
The laffter jest kep' ripplin' 'roun' an' teacher couldn't quell it,

Fur when he give out "charity" ole Hiram couldn't spell it.
But laffin' 's ketchin' an' it throwed some others off their bases,
An' folks 'u'd miss the very word that seemed to fit their cases.
Why, fickle little Jessie Lee come near the house upsettin'
By puttin' in a double "kay" to spell the word "coquettin'."
An' when it come to Cyrus Jones, it tickled me all over—
Him settin' up to Mandy Smith an' got sot down on "lover."
But Lawyer Jones of all gone men did shorely look the gonest,
When he found out that he'd furgot to put the "h" in "honest."
An' Parson Brown, whose sermons were too long fur toleration,
Caused lots o' smiles by missin' when they give out "condensation."
So one by one they giv' it up—the big words kep' a-landin',
Till me an' Nettie Gray was left, the only ones a-standin',
An' then my inward strife began—I guess my mind was petty!—

I did so want that spellin'-book; but then to spell down Nettie
Jest sort o' went ag'in my grain—I somehow couldn't do it,
An' when I git a notion fixed, I'm great on stickin' to it.
So when they giv' the next word out—I hadn't otter tell it,
But then 't was all fur Nettie's sake—I missed so's she could spell it.
She spelt the word, then looked at me so lovin'-like an' mello',
I tell you 't sent a hunderd pins a-shootin' through a fello'.
O' course I had to stand the jokes an' chaffin' of the fello's,
But when they handed her the book I vow I wasn't jealous.
We sung a hymn, an' Parson Brown dismissed us like he otter,
Fur, la! he'd learned a thing er two an' made his blessin' shorter.
'Twas late an' cold when we got out, but Nettie liked cold weather,
An' so did I, so we agreed we'd jest walk home together.
We both wuz silent, fur of words we nuther had a surplus,
'Till she spoke out quite sudden like, "You missed that word on
    purpose."
Well, I declare it frightened me; at first I tried denyin',
But Nettie, she jest smiled an' smiled, she knowed that I was lyin'.
Sez she: "That book is yourn by right;" sez I: "It never could be—
I—I—you—ah—" an' there I stuck, an' well she understood me.
So we agreed that later on when age had giv' us tether,
We'd jine our lots an' settle down to own that book together.

Keep A-Pluggin' Away

I've a humble little motto
That is homely, though it's true,—
Keep a-pluggin' away.
It's a thing when I've an object
That I always try to do,—
Keep a-pluggin' away.
When you've rising storms to quell,
When opposing waters swell,
It will never fail to tell,—
Keep a-pluggin' away.

If the hills are high before
And the paths are hard to climb,
Keep a-pluggin' away.
And remember that successes
Come to him who bides his time,—
Keep a-pluggin' away.
From the greatest to the least,
None are from the rule released.
Be thou toiler, poet, priest,
Keep a-pluggin' away.

Delve away beneath the surface,
There is treasure farther down,—
Keep a-pluggin' away.
Let the rain come down in torrents,
Let the threat'ning heavens frown,
Keep a-pluggin' away.
When the clouds have rolled away,
There will come a brighter day
All your labor to repay,—
Keep a-pluggin' away.

There'll be lots of sneers to swallow.
There'll be lots of pain to bear,—
Keep a-pluggin' away.

If you've got your eye on heaven,
Some bright day you'll wake up there,
Keep a-pluggin' away.
Perseverance still is king;
Time its sure reward will bring;
Work and wait unwearying,—
Keep a-pluggin' away.

NIGHT OF LOVE

The moon has left the sky, love,
The stars are hiding now,
And frowning on the world, love,
Night bares her sable brow.
The snow is on the ground, love,
And cold and keen the air is.
I'm singing here to you, love;
You're dreaming there in Paris.

But this is Nature's law, love,
Though just it may not seem,
That men should wake to sing, love;
While maidens sleep and dream.
Them care may not molest, love,
Nor stir them from their slumbers,
Though midnight find the swain, love.
Still halting o'er his numbers.

I watch the rosy dawn, love,
Come stealing up the east,
While all things round rejoice, love,
That Night her reign has ceased.
The lark will soon be heard, love,
And on his way be winging;
When Nature's poets wake, love,
Why should a man be singing?

Columbian Ode

I

Four hundred years ago a tangled waste
Lay sleeping on the west Atlantic's side;
Their devious ways the Old World's millions traced
Content, and loved, and labored, dared and died.
While students still believed the charts they conned,
And revelled in their thriftless ignorance,
Nor dreamed of other lands that lay beyond
Old Ocean's dense, indefinite expanse.

II

But deep within her heart old Nature knew
That she had once arrayed, at Earth's behest,
Another offspring, fine and fair to view,—
The chosen suckling of the mother's breast.
The child was wrapped in vestments soft and fine,
Each fold a work of Nature's matchless art;
The mother looked on it with love divine,
And strained the loved one closely to her heart.
And there it lay, and with the warmth grew strong
And hearty, by the salt sea breezes fanned,
Till Time with mellowing touches passed along,
And changed the infant to a mighty land.

III

But men knew naught of this, till there arose
That mighty mariner, the Genoese,
Who dared to try, in spite of fears and foes,
The unknown fortunes of unsounded seas.
O noblest of Italia's sons, thy bark
Went not alone into that shrouding night!
O dauntless darer of the rayless dark,
The world sailed with thee to eternal light!

The deer-haunts that with game were crowded then
Today are tilled and cultivated lands;
The schoolhouse tow'rs where Bruin had his den,
And where the wigwam stood the chapel stands;
The place that nurtured men of savage mien
Now teems with men of Nature's noblest types;
Where moved the forest-foliage banner green,
Now flutters in the breeze the stars and stripes!

A BORDER BALLAD

Oh, I haven't got long to live, for we all
Die soon, e'en those who live longest;
And the poorest and weakest are taking their chance
Along with the richest and strongest.
So it's heigho for a glass and a song,
And a bright eye over the table,
And a dog for the hunt when the game is flush.
And the pick of a gentleman's stable.

There is Dimmock o' Dune, he was here yesternight,
But he's rotting today on Glen Arragh;
'Twas the hand o' MacPherson that gave him the blow,
And the vultures shall feast on his marrow.
But it's heigho for a brave old song
And a glass while we are able;
Here's a health to death and another cup
To the bright eye over the table.

I can show a broad back and a jolly deep chest,
But who argues now on appearance?
A blow or a thrust or a stumble at best
May send me today to my clearance.
Then it's heigho for the things I love,
My mother'll be soon wearing sable,
But give me my horse and my dog and my glass,
And a bright eye over the table.

An Easy-Goin' Feller

Ther' ain't no use in all this strife,
An' hurryin', pell-mell, right thro' life.
I don't believe in goin' too fast
To see what kind o' road you've passed.
It ain't no mortal kind o' good,
'N' I wouldn't hurry ef I could.
I like to jest go joggin' 'long,
To limber up my soul with song;
To stop awhile 'n' chat the men.
'N' drink some cider now an' then.

Do' want no boss a-standin' by
To see me work; I allus try
To do my dooty right straight up,
An' earn what fills my plate an' cup.
An' ez fur boss, I'll be my own,
I like to jest be let alone,
To plough my strip an' tend my bees,
An' do jest like I doggoned please.
My head's all right, an' my heart's meller,
But I'm a easy-goin' feller.

A Negro Love Song

Seen my lady home las' night,
Jump back, honey, jump back.
Hel' huh han' an' sque'z it tight,
Jump back, honey, jump back.
Hyeahd huh sigh a little sigh,
Seen a light gleam f'om huh eye,
An' a smile go flittin' by—
Jump back, honey, jump back.

Hyeahd de win' blow thoo de pine,
Jump back, honey, jump back.
Mockin'-bird was singin' fine,
Jump back, honey, jump back.
An' my hea't was beatin' so,
When I reached my lady's do'.
Dat I couldn't ba' to go—
Jump back, honey, jump back.

Put my ahm aroun' huh wais',
Jump back, honey, jump back.
Raised huh lips an' took a tase,
Jump back, honey, jump back
Love me, honey, love me true?
Love me well ez I love you?
An' she answe'd, "'Cose I do"—
Jump back, honey, jump back.

The Dilettante: A Modern Type

He scribbles some in prose and verse,
And now and then he prints it;
He paints a little,—gathers some
Of Nature's gold and mints it.

He plays a little, sings a song,
Acts tragic roles, or funny;
He does, because his love is strong,
But not, oh, not for money!

He studies almost everything
From social art to science;
A thirsty mind, a flowing spring,
Demand and swift compliance.

He looms above the sordid crowd—
At least through friendly lenses;
While his mamma looks pleased and proud,
And kindly pays expenses.

BY THE STREAM

By the stream I dream in calm delight, and watch as in a glass,
How the clouds like crowds of snowy-hued and white-robed maidens
    pass,
And the water into ripples breaks and sparkles as it spreads,
Like a host of armored knights with silver helmets on their heads.
And I deem the stream an emblem fit of human life may go,
For I find a mind may sparkle much and yet but shallows show,
And a soul may glow with myriad lights and wondrous mysteries,
When it only lies a dormant thing and mirrors what it sees.

The Colored Soldiers

If the muse were mine to tempt it
And my feeble voice were strong,
If my tongue were trained to measures,
I would sing a stirring song.
I would sing a song heroic
Of those noble sons of Ham,
Of the gallant colored soldiers
Who fought for Uncle Sam!

In the early days you scorned them,
And with many a flip and flout
Said "These battles are the white man's,
And the whites will fight them out."
Up the hills you fought and faltered,
In the vales you strove and bled,
While your ears still heard the thunder
Of the foes' advancing tread.

Then distress fell on the nation,
And the flag was drooping low;
Should the dust pollute your banner?
No! the nation shouted, No!
So when War, in savage triumph,
Spread abroad his funeral pall—
Then you called the colored soldiers,
And they answered to your call.

And like hounds unleashed and eager
For the life blood of the prey,
Spring they forth and bore them bravely
In the thickest of the fray.
And where'er the fight was hottest,
Where the bullets fastest fell,
There they pressed unblanched and fearless
At the very mouth of hell.

Ah, they rallied to the standard
To uphold it by their might;
None were stronger in the labors,
None were braver in the fight.
From the blazing breach of Wagner
To the plains of Olustee,
They were foremost in the fight
Of the battles of the free.

And at Pillow! God have mercy
On the deeds committed there,
And the souls of those poor victims
Sent to Thee without a prayer.
Let the fulness of Thy pity
O'er the hot wrought spirits sway
Of the gallant colored soldiers
Who fell fighting on that day!

Yes, the Blacks enjoy their freedom,
And they won it dearly, too;
For the life blood of their thousands
Did the southern fields bedew.
In the darkness of their bondage,
In the depths of slavery's night,
Their muskets flashed the dawning,
And they fought their way to light.

They were comrades then and brothers.
Are they more or less today?
They were good to stop a bullet
And to front the fearful fray.
They were citizens and soldiers,
When rebellion raised its head;
And the traits that made them worthy,—
Ah! those virtues are not dead.

They have shared your nightly vigils,
They have shared your daily toil;
And their blood with yours commingling

Has enriched the Southern soil.
They have slept and marched and suffered
'Neath the same dark skies as you,
They have met as fierce a foeman,
And have been as brave and true.

And their deeds shall find a record
In the registry of Fame;
For their blood has cleansed completely
Every blot of Slavery's shame.
So all honor and all glory
To those noble sons of Ham—
The gallant colored soldiers
Who fought for Uncle Sam!

Nature and Art

To My Friend Charles Booth Nettleton

I

The young queen Nature, ever sweet and fair,
Once on a time fell upon evil days.
From hearing oft herself discussed with praise,
There grew within her heart the longing rare
To see herself; and every passing air
The warm desire fanned into lusty blaze.
Full oft she sought this end by devious ways,
But sought in vain, so fell she in despair,
For none within her train nor by her side
Could solve the task or give the envied boon.
So day and night, beneath the sun and moon,
She wandered to and fro unsatisfied,
Till Art came by, a blithe inventive elf,
And made a glass wherein she saw herself.

II

Enrapt, the queen gazed on her glorious self,
Then trembling with the thrill of sudden thought,
Commanded that the skilful wight be brought
That she might dower him with lands and pelf.
Then out upon the silent sea-lapt shelf
And up the hills and on the downs they sought
Him who so well and wondrously had wrought;
And with much search found and brought home the elf.
But he put by all gifts with sad replies,
And from his lips these words flowed forth like wine:
"O queen, I want no gift but thee," he said.
She heard and looked on him with love-lit eyes,
Gave him her hand, low murmuring, "I am thine,"
And at the morrow's dawning they were wed.

After While

A Poem of Faith

I think that though the clouds be dark,
That though the waves dash o'er the bark.
Yet after while the light will come,
And in calm waters safe at home
The bark will anchor.
Weep not, my sad-eyed, gray-robed maid.
Because your fairest blossoms fade,
That sorrow still o'erruns your cup,
And even though you root them up,
The weeds grow ranker.

For after while your tears shall cease,
And sorrow shall give way to peace;
The flowers shall bloom, the weeds shall die,
And in that faith seen, by and by
Thy woes shall perish.
Smile at old Fortune's adverse tide,
Smile when the scoffers sneer and chide.
Oh, not for you the gems that pale,
And not for you the flowers that fail;
Let this thought cherish:

That after while the clouds will part,
And then with joy the waiting heart
Shall feel the light come stealing in,
That drives away the cloud of sin
And breaks its power.
And you shall burst your chrysalis,
And wing away to realms of bliss,
Untrammelled, pure, divinely free,
Above all earth's anxiety
From that same hour.

PAUL LAURENCE DUNBAR

The Ol' Tunes

You kin talk about yer anthems
An' yer arias an' sich,
An' yer modern choir-singin'
That you think so awful rich;
But you orter heerd us youngsters
In the times now far away,
A-singin' o' the ol' tunes
In the ol'-fashioned way.

There was some of us sung treble
An' a few of us growled bass,
An' the tide o' song flowed smoothly
With its 'comp'niment o' grace;
There was spirit in that music,
An' a kind o' solemn sway,
A-singin' o' the ol' tunes
In the ol'-fashioned way.

I remember oft o' standin'
In my homespun pantaloons—
On my face the bronze an' freckles
O' the suns o' youthful Junes—
Thinkin' that no mortal minstrel
Ever chanted sich a lay
As the ol' tunes we was singin'
In the ol'-fashioned way.

The boys 'ud always lead ,as,
An' the girls 'ud all chime in,
Till the sweetness o' the singin'
Robbed the list'nin' soul o' sin;
An' I used to tell the parson
'Twas as good to sing as pray,
When the people sung the ol' tunes
In the ol'-fashioned way.

How I long ag'in to hear 'em
Pourin' forth from soul to soul,
With the treble high an' meller,
An' the bass's mighty roll;
But the times is very diff'rent,
An' the music heerd today
Ain't the singin' o' the ol' tunes
In the ol'-fashioned way.

Little screechin' by a woman,
Little squawkin' by a man,
Then the organ's twiddle-twaddle,
Jest the empty space to span,—
An' ef you should even think it,
'T isn't proper fur to say
That you want to hear the ol' tunes
In the ol'-fashioned way.

But I think that some bright mornin',
When the toils of life air o'er,
An' the sun o' heaven arisin'
Glads with light the happy shore,
I shall hear the angel chorus,
In the realms of endless day,
A-singin' o' the ol' tunes
In the ol'-fashioned way.

Melancholia

Silently without my window,
Tapping gently at the pane,
Falls the rain.
Through the trees sighs the breeze
Like a soul in pain.
Here alone I sit and weep;
Thought hath banished sleep.

Wearily I sit and listen
To the water's ceaseless drip.
To my lip
Fate turns up the bitter cup,
Forcing me to sip;
'Tis a bitter, bitter drink,
Thus I sit and think,—

Thinking things unknown and awful,
Thoughts on wild, uncanny themes,
Waking dreams.
Spectres dark, corpses stark,
Show the gaping seams
Whence the cold and cruel knife
Stole away their life.

Bloodshot eyes all strained and staring,
Gazing ghastly into mine;
Blood like wine
On the brow—clotted now—
Shows death's dreadful sign.
Lonely vigil still I keep;
Would that I might sleep!

Still, oh, still, my brain is whirling!
Still runs on my stream of thought;
I am caught
In the net fate hath set.

Mind and soul are brought
To destruction's very brink;
Yet I can but think!

Eyes that look into the future,—
Peeping forth from out my mind,
They will find
Some new weight, soon or late,
On my soul to bind,
Crushing all its courage out,—
Heavier than doubt.

Dawn, the Eastern monarch's daughter,
Rising from her dewy bed,
Lays her head
'Gainst the clouds' sombre shrouds
Now half fringed with red.
O'er the land she 'gins to peep;
Come, O gentle Sleep!

Hark! the morning cock is crowing;
Dreams, like ghosts, must hie away;
'Tis the day.
Rosy morn now is born;
Dark thoughts may not stay.
Day my brain from foes will keep;
Now, my soul, I sleep.

The Wooing

A Youth went faring up and down,
Alack and well-a-day.
He fared him to the market town,
Alack and well-a-day.
And there he met a maiden fair,
With hazel eyes and auburn hair;
His heart went from him then and there,
Alack and well-a-day.

She posies sold right merrily,
Alack and well-a-day;
But not a flower was fair as she,
Alack and well-a-day.
He bought a rose and sighed a sigh,
"Ah, dearest maiden, would that I
Might dare the seller too to buy!"
Alack and well-a-day.

She tossed her head, the coy coquette,
Alack and well-a-day.
"I'm not, sir, in the market yet,"
Alack and well-a-day.
"Your love must cool upon a shelf;
Tho' much I sell for gold and pelf,
I'm yet too young to sell myself,"
Alack and well-a-day.

The youth was filled with sorrow sore,
Alack and well-a-day;
And looked he at the maid once more,
Alack and well-a-day.
Then loud he cried, "Fair maiden, if
Too young to sell, now as I live,
You're not too young yourself to give,"
Alack and well-a-day.

The little maid cast down her eyes,
Alack and well-a-day,
And many a flush began to rise,
Alack and well-a-day.
"Why, since you are so bold," she said,
"I doubt not you are highly bred,
So take me!" and the twain were wed,
Alack and well-a-day.

Merry Autumn

It's all a farce,—these tales they tell
About the breezes sighing,
And moans astir o'er field and dell,
Because the year is dying.

Such principles are most absurd,—
I care not who first taught 'em;
There's nothing known to beast or bird
To make a solemn autumn.

In solemn times, when grief holds sway
With countenance distressing,
You'll note the more of black and gray
Will then be used in dressing.

Now purple tints are all around;
The sky is blue and mellow;
And e'en the grasses turn the ground
From modest green to yellow.

The seed burrs all with laughter crack
On featherweed and jimson;
And leaves that should be dressed in black
Are all decked out in crimson.

A butterfly goes winging by;
A singing bird comes after;
And Nature, all from earth to sky,
Is bubbling o'er with laughter.

The ripples wimple on the rills,
Like sparkling little lasses;
The sunlight runs along the hills,
And laughs among the grasses.

The earth is just so full of fun
It really can't contain it;
And streams of mirth so freely run
The heavens seem to rain it.

Don't talk to me of solemn days
In autumn's time of splendor,
Because the sun shows fewer rays,
And these grow slant and slender.

Why, it's the climax of the year,—
The highest time of living!—
Till naturally its bursting cheer
Just melts into thanksgiving.

When De Co'n Pone's Hot

Dey is times in life when Nature
Seems to slip a cog an' go,
Jes' a-rattlin' down creation,
Lak an ocean's overflow;
When de worl' jes' stahts a-spinnin'
Lak a picaninny's top,
An' yo' cup o' joy is brimmin'
'Twell it seems about to slop,
An' you feel jes' lak a racah,
Dat is trainin' fu' to trot—
When yo' mammy says de blessin'
An' de co'n pone's hot.

When you set down at de table,
Kin' o' weary lak an' sad,
An' you'se jes' a little tiahed
An' purhaps a little mad;
How yo' gloom tu'ns into gladness,
How yo' joy drives out de doubt
When de oven do' is opened,
An' de smell comes po'in' out;
Why, de 'lectric light o' Heaven
Seems to settle on de spot,
When yo' mammy says de blessin'
An' de co'n pone's hot.

When de cabbage pot is steamin'
An' de bacon good an' fat,
When de chittlins is a-sputter'n'
So's to show you whah dey's at;
Tek away yo' sody biscuit,
Tek away yo' cake an' pie,
Fu' de glory time is comin',
An' it's 'proachin' mighty nigh,
An' you want to jump an' hollah,
Dough you know you'd bettah not,

When yo' mammy says de blessin',
An' de co'n pone's hot.

I have hyeahd o' lots o' sermons,
An' I've hyeahd o' lots o' prayers,
An' I've listened to some singin'
Dat has tuck me up de stairs
Of de Glory-Lan' an' set me
Jes' below de Mahstah's th'one,
An' have lef' my hea't a-singin'
In a happy aftah tone;
But dem wu'ds so sweetly murmured
Seem to tech de softes' spot,
When my mammy says de blessin',
An' de co'n pone's hot.

Ballad

I know my love is true,
And oh the day is fair.
The sky is dear and blue,
The flowers are rich of hue,
The air I breathe is rare,
I have no grief or care;
For my own love is true,
And oh the day is fair.

My love is false I find,
And oh the day is dark.
Blows sadly down the wind,
While sorrow holds my mind;
I do not hear the lark,
For quenched is life's dear spark,—
My love is false I find,
And oh the day is dark!

For love doth make the day
Or dark or doubly bright;
Her beams along the way
Dispel the gloom and gray.
She lives and all is bright,
She dies and life is night.
For love doth make the day,
Or dark or doubly bright.

The Change Has Come

The change has come, and Helen sleeps—
Not sleeps; but wakes to greater deeps
Of wisdom, glory, truth, and light,
Than ever blessed her seeking sight,
In this low, long, lethargic night,
Worn out with strife
Which men call life.

The change has come, and who would say
"I would it were not come today"?
What were the respite till tomorrow?
Postponement of a certain sorrow,
From which each passing day would borrow!
Let grief be dumb,
The change has come.

Comparison

The sky of brightest gray seems dark
To one whose sky was ever white.
To one who never knew a spark,
Thro' all his life, of love or light,
The grayest cloud seems over-bright.

The robin sounds a beggar's note
Where one the nightingale has heard,
But he for whom no silver throat
Its liquid music ever stirred,
Deems robin still the sweetest bird.

A Corn-Song

On the wide veranda white,
In the purple failing light,
Sits the master while the sun is lowly burning;
And his dreamy thoughts are drowned
In the softly flowing sound
Of the corn-songs of the field-hands slow returning.

Oh, we hoe de co'n
Since de ehly mo'n;
Now de sinkin' sun
Says de day is done.
O'er the fields with heavy tread,
Light of heart and high of head,
Though the halting steps be labored, slow, and weary;
Still the spirits brave and strong
Find a comforter in song,
And their corn-song rises ever loud and cheery.

Oh, we hoe de co'n
Since de ehly mo'n;
Now de sinkin' sun
Says de day is done.
To the master in his seat,
Comes the burden, full and sweet,
Of the mellow minor music growing clearer,
As the toilers raise the hymn,
Thro' the silence dusk and dim,
To the cabin's restful shelter drawing nearer.

Oh, we hoe de co'n
Since de ehly mo'n;
Now de sinkin' sun
Says de day is done.
And a tear is in the eye
Of the master sitting by,
As he listens to the echoes low-replying

To the music's fading calls
As it faints away and falls
Into silence, deep within the cabin dying.

Oh, we hoe de co'n
Since de ehly mo'n;
Now de sinkin' sun
Says de day is done.

Discovered

Seen you down at chu'ch las' night,
Nevah min', Miss Lucy.
What I mean? oh, dat's all right,
Nevah min', Miss Lucy.
You was sma't ez sma't could be,
But you couldn't hide f'om me.
Ain't I got two eyes to see!
Nevah min', Miss Lucy.

Guess you thought you's awful keen;
Nevah min', Miss Lucy.
Evahthing you done, I seen;
Nevah min', Miss Lucy.
Seen him tek yo' ahm jes' so,
When he got outside de do'—
Oh, I know dat man's yo' beau!
Nevah min', Miss Lucy.

Say now, honey, wha'd he say?—
Nevah min', Miss Lucy!
Keep yo' secrets—dat's yo' way—
Nevah min', Miss Lucy.
Won't tell me an' I'm yo' pal—
I'm gwine tell his othah gal,—
Know huh, too, huh name is Sal;
Nevah min', Miss Lucy!

Disappointed

An old man planted and dug and tended,
Toiling in joy from dew to dew;
The sun was kind, and the rain befriended;
Fine grew his orchard and fair to view.
Then he said: "I will quiet my thrifty fears,
For here is fruit for my failing years."

But even then the storm-clouds gathered,
Swallowing up the azure sky;
The sweeping winds into white foam lathered
The placid breast of the bay, hard by;
Then the spirits that raged in the darkened air
Swept o'er his orchard and left it bare.

The old man stood in the rain, uncaring,
Viewing the place the storm had swept;
And then with a cry from his soul despairing,
He bowed him down to the earth and wept.
But a voice cried aloud from the driving rain;
"Arise, old man, and plant again!"

INVITATION TO LOVE

Come when the nights are bright with stars
Or when the moon is mellow;
Come when the sun his golden bars
Drops on the hay-field yellow.
Come in the twilight soft and gray,
Come in the night or come in the day,
Come, O Love, whene'er you may,
And you are welcome, welcome.

You are sweet, O Love, dear Love,
You are soft as the nesting dove.
Come to my heart and bring it rest
As the bird flies home to its welcome nest.

Come when my heart is full of grief
Or when my heart is merry;
Come with the falling of the leaf
Or with the redd'ning cherry;

Come when the year's first blossom blows,
Come when the summer gleams and glows,
Come with the winter's drifting snows,
And you are welcome, welcome.

He had His Dream

He had his dream, and all through life,
Worked up to it through toil and strife.
Afloat fore'er before his eyes,
It colored for him all his skies:
The storm-cloud dark
Above his bark,
The calm and listless vault of blue
Took on its hopeful hue,
It tinctured every passing beam—
He had his dream.

He labored hard and failed at last,
His sails too weak to bear the blast,
The raging tempests tore away
And sent his beating bark astray.
But what cared he
For wind or sea!
He said, "The tempest will be short,
My bark will come to port."
He saw through every cloud a gleam—
He had his dream.

Good-Night

The lark is silent in his nest,
The breeze is sighing in its flight,
Sleep, Love, and peaceful be thy rest.
Good-night, my love, good-night, good-night.

Sweet dreams' attend thee in thy sleep,
To soothe thy rest till morning's light,
And angels round thee vigil keep.
Good-night, my love, good-night, good-night.

Sleep well, my love, on night's dark breast,
And ease thy soul with slumber bright;
Be joy but thine and I am blest.
Good-night, my love, good-night, good-night.

A Coquette Conquered

Yes, my ha't's ez ha'd ez stone—
Go 'way, Sam, an' lemme 'lone.
No; I ain't gwine change my min'—
Ain't gwine ma'y you—nuffin' de kin'.

Phiny loves you true an' deah?
Go ma'y Phiny; whut I keer?
Oh, you needn't mou'n an' cry—
I don't keer how soon you die.

Got a present! Whut you got?
Somef'n fu' de pan er pot!
Huh! yo' sass do sholy beat—
Think I don't git 'nough to eat?

Whut's dat un'neaf yo' coat?
Looks des lak a little shoat.
'Tain't no possum! Bless de Lamb!
Yes, it is, you rascal, Sam!

Gin it to me; whut you say?
Ain't you sma't now! Oh, go 'way!
Possum do look mighty nice,
But you ax too big a price.

Tell me, is you talkin' true,
Dat's de gal's whut ma'ies you?
Come back, Sam; now whah's you gwine?
Co'se you knows dat possum's mine!

Nora: A Serenade

Ah, Nora, my Nora, the light fades away,
While Night like a spirit steals up o'er the hills;
The thrash from his tree where he chanted all day,
No longer his music in ecstasy trills.
Then, Nora, be near me; thy presence doth cheer me,
Thine eye hath a gleam that is truer than gold.
I cannot but love thee; so do not reprove me,
If the strength of my passion should make me too bold.

Nora, pride of my heart,—
Rosy cheeks, cherry lips, sparkling with glee,—
Wake from thy slumbers, wherever thou art;
Wake from thy slumbers to me.

Ah, Nora, my Nora, there's love in the air,—
It stirs in the numbers that thrill in my brain;
Oh, sweet, sweet is love with its mingling of care,
Though joy travels only a step before pain.
Be roused from thy slumbers and list to my numbers;
My heart is poured out in this song unto thee.
Oh, be thou not cruel, thou treasure, thou jewel;
Turn thine ear to my pleading and hearken to me.

October

October is the treasurer of the year,
And all the months pay bounty to her store;
The fields and orchards still their tribute bear,
And fill her brimming coffers more and more.
But she, with youthful lavishness,
Spends all her wealth in gaudy dress,
And decks herself in garments bold
Of scarlet, purple, red, and gold.

She heedeth not how swift the hours fly,
But smiles and sings her happy life along;
She only sees above a shining sky;
She only hears the breezes' voice in song.
Her garments trail the woodlands through,
And gather pearls of early dew
That sparkle, till the roguish Sun
Creeps up and steals them every one.

But what cares she that jewels should be lost,
When all of Nature's bounteous wealth is hers?
Though princely fortunes may have been their cost,
Not one regret her calm demeanor stirs.
Whole-hearted, happy, careless, free,
She lives her life out joyously,
Nor cares when Frost stalks o'er her way
And turns her auburn locks to gray.

A Summer's Night

The night is dewy as a maiden's mouth,
The skies are bright as are a maiden's eyes,
Soft as a maiden's breath the wind that flies
Up from the perfumed bosom of the South.
Like sentinels, the pines stand in the park;
And hither hastening, like rakes that roam,
With lamps to light their wayward footsteps home,
The fireflies come stagg'ring down the dark.

Ships that Pass in the Night

Out in the sky the great dark clouds are massing;
I look far out into the pregnant night,
Where I can hear a solemn booming gun
And catch the gleaming of a random light,
That tells me that the ship I seek is passing, passing.

My tearful eyes my soul's deep hurt are glassing;
For I would hail and check that ship of ships.
I stretch my hands imploring, cry aloud,
My voice falls dead a foot from mine own lips,
And but its ghost doth reach that vessel, passing, passing.
O Earth, O Sky, O Ocean, both surpassing,
O heart of mine, O soul that dreads the dark!
Is there no hope for me? Is there no way
That I may sight and check that speeding bark
Which out of sight and sound is passing, passing?

The Delinquent

Goo'-By, Jinks, I got to hump,
Got to mek dis pony jump;
See dat sun a-goin' down
'N' me a-foolin' hyeah in town!
Git up, Suke—go long!

Guess Mirandy'll think I's tight,
Me not home an' comin' on night.
What's dat stan'in' by de fence?
Pshaw! why don't I lu'n some sense?
Git up, Suke—go long!

Guess I spent down dah at Jinks'
Mos' a dollah fur de drinks.
Bless yo'r soul, you see dat star?
Lawd, but won't Mirandy rar?
Git up, Suke—go long!

Went dis mo'nin', hyeah it's night,
Dab's de cabin dah in sight.
Who's dat stan'in' in de do'?
Dat must be Mirandy, sho',
Git up, Suke—go long!

Got de close-stick in huh han',
Dat look funny, goodness lan',
Sakes alibe, but she look glum!
Hyeah, Mirandy, hyeah I come!
Git up, Suke—go long!
Ef 't hadn't a be'n fur you, you slow ole fool,
I'd a' be'n home long fo' now!

Dawn

An angel, robed in spotless white,
Bent down and kissed the sleeping Night.
Night woke to blush; the sprite was gone.
Men saw the blush and called it Dawn.

A Drowsy Day

The air is dark, the sky is gray,
The misty shadows come and go,
And here within my dusky room
Each chair looks ghostly in the gloom.
Outside the rain falls cold and slow—
Half-stinging drops, half-blinding spray.

Each slightest sound is magnified,
For drowsy quiet holds her reign;
The burnt stick in the fireplace breaks,
The nodding cat with start awakes,
And then to sleep drops off again,
Unheeding Towser at her side.

I look far out across the lawn,
Where huddled stand the silly sheep;
My work lies idle at my hands,
My thoughts fly out like scattered strands
Of thread, and on the verge of sleep—
Still half awake—I dream and yawn.

What spirits rise before my eyes!
How various of kind and form!
Sweet memories of days long past,
The dreams of youth that could not last,
Each smiling calm, each raging storm,
That swept across my early skies.

Half seen, the bare, gaunt-fingered boughs
Before my window sweep and sway,
And chafe in tortures of unrest.
My chin sinks down upon my breast;
I cannot work on such a day,
But only sit and dream and drowse.

DIRGE

Place this bunch of mignonette
In her cold, dead hand;
When the golden sun is set,
Where the poplars stand,
Bury her from sun and day,
Lay my little love away
From my sight.

She was like a modest flower
Blown in sunny June,
Warm as sun at noon's high hour,
Chaster than the moon.
Ah, her day was brief and bright,
Earth has lost a star of light;
She is dead.

Softly breathe her name to me,—
Ah, I loved her so.
Gentle let your tribute be;
None may better know
Her true worth than I who weep
O'er her as she lies asleep—
Soft asleep.

Lay these lilies on her breast,
They are not more white
Than the soul of her, at rest
'Neath their petals bright.
Chant your aves soft and low,
Solemn be your tread and slow,—
She is dead.

Lay her here beneath the grass,
Cool and green and sweet,
Where the gentle brook may pass
Crooning at her feet.

Nature's bards shall come and sing,
And the fairest flowers shall spring
Where she lies.

Safe above the water's swirl,
She has crossed the bar;
Earth has lost a precious pearl,
Heaven has gained a star,
That shall ever sing and shine,
Till it quells this grief of mine
For my love.

Hymn

When storms arise
And dark'ning skies
About me threat'ning lower,
To thee, O Lord, I raise mine eyes,
To thee my tortured spirit flies
For solace in that hour.

Thy mighty arm
Will let no harm
Come near me nor befall me;
Thy voice shall quiet my alarm,
When life's great battle waxeth warm—
No foeman shall appall me.

Upon thy breast
Secure I rest,
From sorrow and vexation;
No more by sinful cares oppressed,
But in thy presence ever blest,
O God of my salvation.

PREPARATION

The little bird sits in the nest and sings
A shy, soft song to the morning light;
And it flutters a little and prunes its wings.
The song is halting and poor and brief,
And the fluttering wings scarce stir a leaf;
But the note is a prelude to sweeter things,
And the busy bill and the flutter slight
Are proving the wings for a bolder flight!

The Deserted Plantation

Oh, de grubbin'-hoe's a-rustin' in de co'nah,
An' de plow's a-tumblin' down in de fiel',
While de whippo'will's a-wailin' lak a mou'nah
When his stubbo'n hea't is tryin' ha'd to yiel'.

In de furrers whah de co'n was allus wavin',
Now de weeds is growin' green an' rank an' tall;
An' de swallers roun' de whole place is a-bravin'
Lak dey thought deir folks had allus owned it all.

An' de big house stan's all quiet lak an' solemn,
Not a blessed soul in pa'lor, po'ch, er lawn;
Not a guest, ner not a ca'iage lef' to haul 'em,
Fu' de ones dat tu'ned de latch-string out air gone.

An' de banjo's voice is silent in de qua'ters,
D' ain't a hymn ner co'n-song ringin' in de air;
But de murmur of a branch's passin' waters
Is de only soun' dat breks de stillness dere.

Whah's de da'kies, dem dat used to be a-dancin'
Evry night befo' de ole cabin do'?
Whah's de chillun, dem dat used to be a-prancin'
Er a-rollin' in de san' er on de flo'?

Whah's ole Uncle Mordecai an' Uncle Aaron?
Whah's Aunt Doshy, Sam, an' Kit, an' all de res'?
Whah's ole Tom de da'ky fiddlah, how's he farin'?
Whah's de gals dat used to sing an' dance de bes'?

Gone! not one o' dem is lef' to tell de story;
Dey have lef de deah ole place to fall away.
Couldn't one o' dem dat seed it in its glory
Stay to watch it in de hour of decay?

Dey have lef' de ole plantation to de swallers,
But it hol's in me a lover till de las';
Fu' I fin' hyeah in de memory dat follers
All dat loved me an' dat I loved in de pas'.

So I'll stay an' watch de deah ole place an' tend it
Ez I used to in de happy days gone by.
'Twell de othah Mastah thinks it's time to end it,
An' calls me to my qua'ters in de sky.

The Secret

What says the wind to the waving trees?
What says the wave to the river?
What means the sigh in the passing breeze?
Why do the rushes quiver?
Have you not heard the fainting cry
Of the flowers that said "Good-bye, good-bye"?

List how the gray dove moans and grieves
Under the woodland cover;
List to the drift of the falling leaves,
List to the wail of the lover.
Have you not caught the message heard
Already by wave and breeze and bird?

Come, come away to the river's bank,
Come in the early morning;
Come when the grass with dew is dank,
There you will find the warning—
A hint in the kiss of the quickening air
Of the secret that birds and breezes bear.

The Wind and the Sea

I stood by the shore at the death of day,
As the sun sank flaming red;
And the face of the waters that spread away
Was as gray as the face of the dead.

And I heard the cry of the wanton sea
And the moan of the wailing wind;
For love's sweet pain in his heart had he,
But the gray old sea had sinned.

The wind was young and the sea was old,
But their cries went up together;
The wind was warm and the sea was cold,
For age makes wintry weather.

So they cried aloud and they wept amain,
Till the sky grew dark to hear it;
And out of its folds crept the misty rain,
In its shroud, like a troubled spirit.

For the wind was wild with a hopeless love,
And the sea was sad at heart
At many a crime that he wot of,
Wherein he had played his part.

He thought of the gallant ships gone down
By the will of his wicked waves;
And he thought how the churchyard in the town
Held the sea-made widows' graves.

The wild wind thought of the love he had left
Afar in an Eastern land,
And he longed, as long the much bereft,
For the touch of her perfumed hand.

In his winding wail and his deep-heaved sigh
His aching grief found vent;
While the sea looked up at the bending sky
And murmured: "I repent."

But e'en as he spoke, a ship came by,
That bravely ploughed the main,
And a light came into the sea's green eye,
And his heart grew hard again.

Then he spoke to the wind: "Friend, seest thou not
Yon vessel is eastward bound?
Pray speed with it to the happy spot
Where thy loved one may be found."

And the wind rose up in a dear delight,
And after the good ship sped;
But the crafty sea by his wicked might
Kept the vessel ever ahead.

Till the wind grew fierce in his despair,
And white on the brow and lip.
He tore his garments and tore his hair,
And fell on the flying ship.

And the ship went down, for a rock was there,
And the sailless sea loomed black;
While burdened again with dole and care,
The wind came moaning back.

And still he moans from his bosom hot
Where his raging grief lies pent,
And ever when the ships come not,
The sea says: "I repent,"

Riding to Town

When labor is light and the morning is fair,
I find it a pleasure beyond all compare
To hitch up my nag and go hurrying down
And take Katie May for a ride into town;
For bumpety-bump goes the wagon,
But tra-la-la-la our lay.
There's joy in a song as we rattle along
In the light of the glorious day.

A coach would be fine, but a spring wagon's good;
My jeans are a match for Kate's gingham and hood;
The hills take us up and the vales take us down,
But what matters that? we are tiding to town,
And bumpety-bump goes the wagon,
But tra-la-la-la sing we.
There's never a care may live in the air
That is filled with the breath of our glee.

And after we've started, there's naught can repress
The thrill of our hearts in their wild happiness;
The heavens may smile or the heavens may frown,
And it's all one to us when we're riding to town.
For bumpety-bump goes the wagon,
But tra-la-la-la we shout,
For our hearts they are clear and there's nothing to fear,
And we've never a pain nor a doubt.

The wagon is weak and the roadway is rough,
And tho' it is long it is not long enough,
For mid all my ecstasies this is the crown
To sit beside Katie and ride into town,
When bumpety-bump goes the wagon,
But tra-la-la-la our song;
And if I had my way, I'd be willing to pay
If the road could be made twice as long.

We Wear the Mask

We wear the mask that grins and lies,
It hides our cheeks and shades our eyes,—
This debt we pay to human guile;
With torn and bleeding hearts we smile,
And mouth with myriad subtleties.

Why should the world be over-wise,
In counting all our tears and sighs?
Nay, let them only see us, while
We wear the mask.

We smile, but, O great Christ, our cries
To thee from tortured souls arise.
We sing, but oh the clay is vile
Beneath our feet, and long the mile;
But let the world dream otherwise,
We wear the mask!

The Meadow Lark

Though the winds be dank,
And the sky be sober,
And the grieving Day
In a mantle gray
Hath let her waiting maiden robe her,—
All the fields along
I can hear the song
Of the meadow lark,
As she flits and flutters,
And laughs at the thunder when it mutters.
O happy bird, of heart most gay
To sing when skies are gray!

When the clouds are full,
And the tempest master
Lets the loud winds sweep
From his bosom deep
Like heralds of some dire disaster,
Then the heart alone
To itself makes moan;
And the songs come slow,
While the tears fall fleeter,
And silence than song by far seems sweeter.
Oh, few are they along the way
Who sing when skies are gray!

PAUL LAURENCE DUNBAR

ONE LIFE

Oh, I am hurt to death, my Love;
The shafts of Fate have pierced my striving heart,
And I am sick and weary of
The endless pain and smart.
My soul is weary of the strife,
And chafes at life, and chafes at life.

Time mocks me with fair promises;
A blooming future grows a barren past,
Like rain my fair full-blossomed trees
Unburden in the blast.
The harvest fails on grain and tree,
Nor comes to me, nor comes to me.

The stream that bears my hopes abreast
Turns ever from my way its pregnant tide.
My laden boat, torn from its rest,
Drifts to the other side.
So all my hopes are set astray,
And drift away, and drift away.

The lark sings to me at the morn,
And near me wings her skyward-soaring flight;
But pleasure dies as soon as born,
The owl takes up the night,
And night seems long and doubly dark;
I miss the lark, I miss the lark.

Let others labor as they may,
I'll sing and sigh alone, and write my line.
Their fate is theirs, or grave or gay,
And mine shall still be mine.
I know the world holds joy and glee,
But not for me,—'t is not for me.

Changing Time

The cloud looked in at the window,
And said to the day, "Be dark!"
And the roguish rain tapped hard on the pane,
To stifle the song of the lark.

The wind sprang up in the tree tops
And shrieked with a voice of death,
But the rough-voiced breeze, that shook the trees,
Was touched with a violet's breath.

PAUL LAURENCE DUNBAR

Dead

A Knock is at her door, but she is weak;
Strange dews have washed the paint streaks from her cheek;
She does not rise, but, ah, this friend is known,
And knows that he will find her all alone.
So opens he the door, and with soft tread
Goes straightway to the richly curtained bed.
His soft hand on her dewy head he lays.
A strange white light she gives him for his gaze.
Then, looking on the glory of her charms,
He crushes her resistless in his arms.

Stand back! look not upon this bold embrace,
Nor view the calmness of the wanton's face;
With joy unspeakable and 'bated breath,
She keeps her last, long liaison with death!

A CONFIDENCE

Uncle John, he makes me tired;
Thinks 'at he's jest so all-fired
Smart, 'at he kin pick up, so,
Ever'thing he wants to know.
Tried to ketch me up last night,
But you bet I wouldn't bite.
I jest kep' the smoothes' face,
But I led him sich a chase,
Couldn't corner me, you bet—
I skipped all the traps he set.
Makin' out he wan'ed to know
Who was this an' that girl's beau;
So's he'd find out, don't you see,
Who was goin' 'long with me.
But I answers jest ez sly,
An' I never winks my eye,
Tell he hollers with a whirl,
"Look here, ain't you got a girl?"
Y' ought 'o seen me spread my eyes,
Like he'd took me by surprise,
An' I said, "Oh, Uncle John,
Never thought o' havin' one."
An' somehow that seemed to tickle
Him an' he shelled out a nickel.
Then you ought to seen me leave
Jest a-laffin' in my sleeve.
Fool him—well, I guess I did;
He ain't on to this here kid.
Got a girl! well, I guess yes,
Got a dozen more or less,
But I got one reely one,
Not no foolin' ner no fun;
Fur I'm sweet on her, you see,
An' I ruther guess 'at she
Must be kinder sweet on me,
So we're keepin' company.

Honest Injun! this is true,
Ever' word I'm tellin' you!
But you won't be sich a scab
Ez to run aroun' an' blab.
Mebbe 't ain't the way with you,
But you know some fellers do.
Spoils a girl to let her know
'At you talk about her so.
Don't you know her? her name's Liz,
Nicest girl in town she is.
Purty? oh, git out, you gilly—
Liz 'ud purt 'nigh knock you silly.
Y' ought 'o see her when she's dressed
All up in her Sunday best,
All the fellers nudgin' me,
An' a-whisperin', gemunee!
Betcher life 'at I feel proud
When she passes by the crowd.
'T's kinder nice to be a-goin'
With a girl 'at makes some showin'—
One you know 'at hain't no snide,
Makes you feel so satisfied.
An' I'll tell you she's a trump,
Never even seen her jump
Like some silly girls 'ud do,
When I'd hide and holler "Boo!"
She'd jest laff an' say "Git out!
What you hollerin' about?"
When some girls 'ud have a fit
That 'un don't git skeered a bit,
Never makes a bit o' row
When she sees a worm er cow.
Them kind's few an' far between;
Bravest girl I ever seen.
Tell you 'nuther thing she'll do,
Mebbe you won't think it's true,
But if she's jest got a dime
She 'll go halvers ever' time.
Ah, you goose, you needn't laff;

That's the kinder girl to have.
If you knowed her like I do,
Guess you'd kinder like her too.
Tell you somep'n' if you'll swear
You won't tell it anywhere.
Oh, you got to cross yer heart
Earnest, truly, 'fore I start.
Well, one day I kissed her cheek;
Gee, but I felt cheap an' weak,
'Cause at first she kinder flared,
'N', gracious goodness! I was scared.
But I needn't been, fer la!
Why, she never told her ma.
That's what I call grit, don't you?
Sich a girl's worth stickin' to.

PAUL LAURENCE DUNBAR

PHYLLIS

Phyllis, ah, Phyllis, my life is a gray day,
Few are my years, but my griefs are not few,
Ever to youth should each day be a May-day,
Warm wind and rose-breath and diamonded dew—
Phyllis, ah, Phyllis, my life is a gray day.

Oh for the sunlight that shines on a May-day!
Only the cloud hangeth over my life.
Love that should bring me youth's happiest heyday
Brings me but seasons of sorrow and strife:
Phyllis, ah, Phyllis, my life is a gray day.

Sunshine or shadow, or gold day or gray day,
Life must be lived as our destinies rule;
Leisure or labor or work day or play day—
Feasts for the famous and fun for the fool;
Phyllis, ah, Phyllis, my life is a gray day.

Right's Security

What if the wind do howl without,
And turn the creaking weather-vane;
What if the arrows of the rain
Do beat against the window-pane?
Art thou not armored strong and fast
Against the sallies of the blast?
Art thou not sheltered safe and well
Against the flood's insistent swell?

What boots it, that thou stand'st alone,
And laughest in the battle's face
When all the weak have fled the place
And let their feet and fears keep pace?
Thou wavest still thine ensign, high,
And shoutest thy loud battle-cry;
Higher than e'er the tempest roared,
It cleaves the silence like a sword.

Right arms and armors, too, that man
Who will not compromise with wrong;
Though single, he must front the throng,
And wage the battle hard and long.
Minorities, since time began,
Have shown the better side of man;
And often in the lists of Time
One man has made a cause sublime!

IF

If life were but a dream, my Love,
And death the waking time;
If day had not a beam, my Love,
And night had not a rhyme,—
A barren, barren world were this
Without one saving gleam;
I'd only ask that with a kiss
You'd wake me from the dream.

If dreaming were the sum of days,
And loving were the bane;
If battling for a wreath of bays
Could soothe a heart in pain,—
I'd scorn the meed of battle's might,
All other aims above
I'd choose the human's higher right,
To suffer and to love!

The Song

My soul, lost in the music's mist,
Roamed, rapt, 'neath skies of amethyst,
The cheerless streets grew summer meads,
The Son of Phœbus spurred his steeds,
And, wand'ring down the mazy tune,
December lost its way in June,
While from a verdant vale I heard
The piping of a love-lorn bird.

A something in the tender strain
Revived an old, long-conquered pain,
And as in depths of many seas,
My heart was drowned in memories.
The tears came welling to my eyes,
Nor could I ask it otherwise;
For, oh! a sweetness seems to last
Amid the dregs of sorrows past.

It stirred a chord that here of late
I'd grown to think could not vibrate.
It brought me back the trust of youth,
The world again was joy and truth.
And Avice, blooming like a bride,
Once more stood trusting at my side.
But still, with bosom desolate,
The 'lorn bird sang to find his mate.

Then there are trees, and lights and stars,
The silv'ry tinkle of guitars;
And throbs again as throbbed that waltz,
Before I knew that hearts were false.
Then like a cold wave on a shore,
Comes silence and she sings no more.
I wake, I breathe, I think again,
And walk the sordid ways of men.

PAUL LAURENCE DUNBAR

Signs of the Times

Air a-gittin' cool an' coolah,
Frost a-comin' in de night,
Hicka' nuts an' wa'nuts fallin',
Possum keepin' out o' sight.
Tu'key struttin' in de ba'nya'd,
Nary step so proud ez his;
Keep on struttin', Mistah Tu'key,
Yo' do' know whut time it is.

Cidah press commence a-squeakin'
Eatin' apples sto'ed away,
Chillun swa'min' 'roun' lak ho'nets,
Huntin' aigs ermung de hay.
Mistah Tu'key keep on gobblin'
At de geese a-flyin' souf,
Oomph! dat bird do' know whut's comin';
Ef he did he'd shet his mouf.
Pumpkin gittin' good an' yallah
Mek me open up my eyes;
Seems lak it's a-lookin' at me
Jes' a-la'in' dah sayin' "Pies."
Tu'key gobbler gwine 'roun' blowin',
Gwine 'roun' gibbin' sass an' slack;
Keep on talkin', Mistah Tu'key,
You ain't seed no almanac.

Fa'mer walkin' th'oo de ba'nya'd
Seein' how things is comin' on,
Sees ef all de fowls, is fatt'nin'—
Good times comin' sho's you bo'n.
Hyeahs dat tu'key gobbler braggin',
Den his face break in a smile—
Nebbah min', you sassy rascal,
He's gwine nab you atter while.

Choppin' suet in de kitchen,
Stonin' raisins in de hall,
Beef a-cookin' fu' de mince meat,
Spices groun'—I smell 'em all.
Look hyeah, Tu'key, stop dat gobblin',
You ain' luned de sense ob feah,
You ol' fool, yo' naik's in dangah,
Do' you know Thanksgibbin's hyeah?

Why Fades a Dream?

Why fades a dream?
An iridescent ray
Flecked in between the tryst
Of night and day.
Why fades a dream?—
Of consciousness the shade
Wrought out by lack of light and made
Upon life's stream.
Why fades a dream?

That thought may thrive,
So fades the fleshless dream;
Lest men should learn to trust
The things that seem.
So fades a dream,
That living thought may grow
And like a waxing star-beam glow
Upon life's stream—
So fades a dream.

The Sparrow

A little bird, with plumage brown,
Beside my window flutters down,
A moment chirps its little strain,
Then taps upon my window-pane,
And chirps again, and hops along,
To call my notice to its song;
But I work on, nor heed its lay,
Till, in neglect, it flies away.

So birds of peace and hope and love
Come fluttering earthward from above,
To settle on life's window-sills,
And ease our load of earthly ills;
But we, in traffic's rush and din
Too deep engaged to let them in,
With deadened heart and sense plod on,
Nor know our loss till they are gone.

Speakin' O' Christmas

Breezes blowin' middlin' brisk,
Snow-flakes thro' the air a-whisk,
Fallin' kind o' soft an' light,
Not enough to make things white,
But jest sorter siftin' down
So's to cover up the brown
Of the dark world's rugged ways
'N' make things look like holidays.
Not smoothed over, but jest specked,
Sorter strainin' fur effect,
An' not quite a-gittin' through
What it started in to do.
Mercy sakes! it does seem queer
Christmas day is 'most nigh here.
Somehow it don't seem to me
Christmas like it used to be,—
Christmas with its ice an' snow,
Christmas of the long ago.
You could feel its stir an' hum
Weeks an' weeks before it come;
Somethin' in the atmosphere
Told you when the day was near,
Didn't need no almanacs;
That was one o' Nature's fac's.
Every cottage decked out gay—
Cedar wreaths an' holly spray—
An' the stores, how they were drest,
Tinsel tell you couldn't rest;
Every winder fixed up pat,
Candy canes, an' things like that;
Noah's arks, an' guns, an' dolls,
An' all kinds o' fol-de-rols.
Then with frosty bells a-chime,
Slidin' down the hills o' time,
Right amidst the fun an' din
Christmas come a-bustlin' in,

Raised his cheery voice to call
Out a welcome to us all.
Hale and hearty, strong an' bluff,
That was Christmas, sure enough.
Snow knee-deep an' coastin' fine,
Frozen mill-ponds all ashine,
Seemin' jest to lay in wait,
Beggin' you to come an' skate.
An' you'd git your gal an' go
Stumpin' cheerily thro' the snow,
Feelin' pleased an' skeert an' warm
'Cause she had a-holt yore arm.
Why, when Christmas come in, we
Spent the whole glad day in glee,
Havin' fun an' feastin' high
An' some courtin' on the sly.
Bustin' in some neighbor's door
An' then suddenly, before
He could give his voice a lift,
Yellin' at him, "Christmas gift."
Now sich things are never heard,
"Merry Christmas" is the word.
But it's only change o' name,
An' means givin' jest the same.
There's too many new-styled ways
Now about the holidays.
I'd jest like once more to see
Christmas like it used to be!

LONESOME

Mother's gone a-visitin' to spend a month er two,
An', oh, the house is lonesome ez a nest whose birds has flew
To other trees to build ag'in; the rooms seem jest so bare
That the echoes run like sperrits from the kitchen to the stair.
The shetters flap more lazy-like 'n what they used to do,
Sence mother's gone a-visitin' to spend a month er two.

We've killed the fattest chicken an' we've cooked her to a turn;
We've made the richest gravy, but I jest don't give a durn
Fur nothin' 'at I drink er eat, er nothin' 'at I see.
The food ain't got the pleasant taste it used to have to me.
They's somep'n' stickin' in my throat ez tight ez hardened glue,
Sence mother's gone a-visitin' to spend a month er two.

The hollyhocks air jest ez pink, they're double ones at that,
An' I wuz prouder of 'em than a baby of a cat.
But now I don't go near 'era, though they nod an' blush at me,
Fur they's somep'n' seems to gall me in their keerless sort o' glee
An' all their fren'ly noddin' an' their blushin' seems to say:
"You're putty lonesome, John, old boy, sence mother's gone away."

The neighbors ain't so fren'ly ez it seems they'd ort to be;
They seem to be a-lookin' kinder sideways like at me,
A-kinder feared they'd tech me off ez ef I wuz a match,
An' all because 'at mother's gone an' I'm a-keepin' batch!
I'm shore I don't do nothin' worse 'n what I used to do
'Fore mother went a-visitin' to spend a month er two.

The sparrers ac's more fearsome like an' won't hop quite so near,
The cricket's chirp is sadder, an' the sky ain't ha'f so clear;
When ev'nin' comes, I set an' smoke tell my eyes begin to swim,
An' things aroun' commence to look all blurred an' faint an' dim.
Well, I guess I'll have to own up 'at I'm feelin' purty blue
Sence mother's gone a-visitin' to spend a month er two.

Growin' Gray

Hello, ole man, you're a-gittin' gray,
An' it beats ole Ned to see the way
'At the crow's feet's a-getherin' aroun' yore eyes;
Tho' it oughtn't to cause me no su'prise,
Fur there's many a sun 'at you've seen rise
An' many a one you've seen go down
Sence yore step was light an' yore hair was brown,
An' storms an' snows have had their way—
Hello, ole man, you're a-gittin' gray.

Hello, ole man, you're a-gittin' gray,
An' the youthful pranks 'at you used to play
Are dreams of a far past long ago
That lie in a heart where the fires burn low—
That has lost the flame though it kept the glow,
An' spite of drivin' snow an' storm,
Beats bravely on forever warm.
December holds the place of May—
Hello, ole man, you're a-gittin' gray.

Hello, ole man, you're a-gittin' gray—
Who cares what the carpin' youngsters say?
For, after all, when the tale is told,
Love proves if a man is young or old!
Old age can't make the heart grow cold
When it does the will of an honest mind;
When it beats with love fur all mankind;
Then the night but leads to a fairer day—
Hello, ole man, you're a-gittin' gray!

To the Memory of Mary Young

God has his plans, and what if we
With our sight be too blind to see
Their full fruition; cannot he,
Who made it, solve the mystery?
One whom we loved has fall'n asleep,
Not died; although her calm be deep,
Some new, unknown, and strange surprise
In Heaven holds enrapt her eyes.

And can you blame her that her gaze
Is turned away from earthly ways,
When to her eyes God's light and love
Have giv'n the view of things above?
A gentle spirit sweetly good,
The pearl of precious womanhood;
Who heard the voice of duty clear,
And found her mission soon and near.

She loved all nature, flowers fair,
The warmth of sun, the kiss of air,
The birds that filled the sky with song,
The stream that laughed its way along.
Her home to her was shrine and throne,
But one love held her not alone;
She sought out poverty and grief,
Who touched her robe and found relief.

So sped she in her Master's work,
Too busy and too brave to shirk,
When through the silence, dusk and dim,
God called her and she fled to him.
We wonder at the early call,
And tears of sorrow can but fall
For her o'er whom we spread the pall;
But faith, sweet faith, is over all.

The house is dust, the voice is dumb,
But through undying years to come,
The spark that glowed within her soul
Shall light our footsteps to the goal.
She went her way; but oh, she trod
The path that led her straight to God.
Such lives as this put death to scorn;
They lose our day to find God's morn.

When Malindy Sings

G'way an' quit dat noise, Miss Lucy—
Put dat music book away;
What's de use to keep on tryin'?
Ef you practise twell you're gray,
You cain't sta't no notes a-flyin'
Lak de ones dat rants and rings
F'om de kitchen to de big woods
When Malindy sings.

You ain't got de nachel o'gans
Fu' to make de soun' come right,
You ain't got de tu'ns an' twistin's
Fu' to make it sweet an' light.
Tell you one thing now, Miss Lucy,
An' I'm tellin' you fu' true,
When hit comes to raal right singin',
'Tain't no easy thing to do.

Easy 'nough fu' folks to hollah,
Lookin' at de lines an' dots,
When dey ain't no one kin sence it,
An' de chune comes in, in spots;
But fu' real melojous music,
Dat jes' strikes yo' hea't and clings,
Jes' you stan' an' listen wif me
When Malindy sings.

Ain't you nevah hyeahd Malindy?
Blessed soul, tek up de cross!
Look hyeah, ain't you jokin', honey?
Well, you don't know whut you los'.
Y'ought to hyeah dat gal a-wa'blin',
Robins, la'ks, an' all dem things,
Heish dey moufs an' hides dey faces
When Malindy sings.

Fiddlin' man jes' stop his fiddlin',
Lay his fiddle on de she'f;
Mockin'-bird quit tryin' to whistle,
'Cause he jes' so shamed hisse'f.
Folks a-playin' on de banjo
Draps dey fingabs on de strings—
Bless yo' soul—fu'gits to move 'em,
When Malindy sings.

She jes' spreads huh mouf and hollahs,
"Come to Jesus," twell you hyeah
Sinnahs' tremblin' steps and voices,
Timid-lak a-drawin' neah;
Den she tu'ns to "Rock of Ages,"
Simply to de cross she clings,
An' you fin' yo' teahs a-drappin'
When Malindy sings.

Who dat says dat humble praises
Wif de Master nevah counts?
Heish yo' mouf, I hyeah dat music,
Ez hit rises up an' mounts—
Floatin' by de hills an' valleys,
Way above dis buryin' sod,
Ez hit makes its way in glory
To de very gates of God!

Oh, hit's sweetah dan de music
Of an edicated band;
An' hit's dearah dan de battle's
Song o' triumph in de lan'.
It seems holier dan evenin'
When de solemn chu'ch bell rings,
Ez I sit an' ca'mly listen
While Malindy sings.

Towsah, stop dat ba'kin', hyeah me!
Mandy, mek dat chile keep still;
Don't you hyeah de echoes callin'

F'om de valley to de hill?
Let me listen, I can hyeah it,
Th'oo de bresh of angel's wings,
Sof' an' sweet, "Swing Low, Sweet Chariot,"
Ez Malindy sings.

The Party

Dey had a gread big pahty down to Tom's de othah night;
Was I dah? You bet! I nevah in my life see sich a sight;
All de folks f'om fou' plantations was invited, an' dey come,
Dey come troopin' thick ez chillun when dey hyeahs a fife an' drum.
Evahbody dressed deir fines'—Heish yo' mouf an' git away,
Ain't seen no sich fancy dressin' sence las' quah'tly meetin' day;
Gals all dressed in silks an' satins, not a wrinkle nor a crease,
Eyes a-battin', teeth a-shinin', haih breshed back ez slick ez grease;
Sku'ts all tucked an' puffed an' ruffled, evah blessed seam an' stitch;
Ef you'd seen 'em wif deir mistus, couldn't swahed to which was which.
Men all dressed up in Prince Alberts, swallertails 'u'd tek yo' bref!
I cain't tell you nothin' 'bout it, y' ought to seen it fu' yo'se'f.
Who was dah? Now who you askin'? How you 'spect I gwine to know?
You mus' think I stood an' counted evahbody at de do'.
Ole man Babah's house-boy Isaac, brung dat gal, Malindy Jane,
Huh a-hannin' to his elbow, him a-struttin' wif a cane;
My, but Hahvey Jones was jealous! seemed to stick him lak a tho'n;
But he laughed with Viney Cahteh, tryin' ha'd to not let on,
But a pusson would 'a' noticed f'om de d'rection of his look,
Dat he was watchin' ev'ry step dat Ike an' Lindy took.
Ike he foun' a cheer an' asked huh: "Won't you set down?" wif a smile,
An' she answe'd up a-bowin', "Oh, I reckon 'tain't wuth while."
Dat was jes' fu' style, I reckon, 'cause she sot down jes' de same,
An' she stayed dah 'twell he fetched huh fu' to jine some so't o' game;
Den I hyeahd huh sayin' propah, ez she riz to go away,
"Oh, you raly mus' excuse me, fu' I hardly keers to play."
But I seen huh in a minute wif de othahs on de flo',
An' dah wasn't any one o' dem a-playin' any mo';
Comin' down de flo' a-bowin' an' a-swayin' an' a-swingin',
Puttin' on huh high-toned mannahs all de time dat she was singin':
"Oh, swing Johnny up an' down, swing him all aroun',
Swing Johnny up an' down, swing him all aroun',
Oh, swing Johnny up an' down, swing him all aroun',
Fa' you well, my dahlin'."
Had to laff at ole man Johnson, he's a caution now, you bet—
Hittin' clost onto a hunderd, but he's spry an' nimble yet;

He 'lowed how a-so't o' gigglin', "I ain't ole, I'll let you see,
D'ain't no use in gittin' feeble, now you youngstahs jes' watch me,"
An' he grabbed ole Aunt Marier—weighs th'ee hunderd mo' er less,
An' he spun huh 'roun' de cabin swingin' Johnny lak de res'.
Evahbody laffed an' hollahed: "Go it! Swing huh, Uncle Jim!"
An' he swung huh too, I reckon, lak a youngstah, who but him.
Dat was bettah 'n young Scott Thomas, tryin' to be so awful smaht.
You know when dey gits to singin' an' dey comes to dat ere paht:
"In some lady's new brick house,
In some lady's gyahden.
Ef you don't let me out, I will jump out,
So fa' you well, my dahlin'."
Den dey's got a circle 'roun' you, an' you's got to break de line;
Well, dat dahky was so anxious, lak to bust hisse'f a-tryin';
Kep' on blund'rin' 'roun' an' foolin' 'twell he giv' one gread big jump,
Broke de line, an' lit head-fo'most in de fiahplace right plump;
Hit 'ad fiah in it, mind you; well, I thought my soul I'd bust,
Tried my best to keep f'om laffin', but hit seemed like die I must!
Y' ought to seen dat man a-scramblin' fore de ashes an' de grime.
Did it bu'n him! Sich a question, why he didn't give it time;
Th'ow'd dem ashes and dem cindahs evah which-a-way I guess,
An' you nevah did, I reckon, clap yo' eyes on sich a mess;
Fu' he sholy made a picter an' a funny one to boot,
Wif his clothes all full o' ashes an' his face all full o' soot.
Well, hit laked to stopped de pahty, an' I reckon lak ez not
Dat it would ef Tom's wife, Mandy, hadn't happened on de spot,
To invite us out to suppah—well, we scrambled to de table,
An' I'd lak to tell you 'bout it—what we had—but I ain't able,
Mention jes' a few things, dough I know I hadn't orter,
Fu' I know 't will staht a hank'rin' an' yo' mouf 'll 'mence to worter.
We had wheat bread white ez cotton an' a egg pone jes like gol',
Hog jole, bilin' hot an' steamin' roasted shoat an' ham sliced cold—
Look out! What's de mattah wif you? Don't be fallin' on de flo';
Ef it's go'n' to 'fect you dat way, I won't tell you nothin' mo'.
Dah now—well, we had hot chittlin's—now you's tryin' ag'in to fall,
Cain't you stan' to hyeah about it? S'pose you'd been an' seed it all;
Seed dem gread big sweet pertaters, layin' by de possum's side,
Seed dat coon in all his gravy, reckon den you'd up and died!
Mandy 'lowed "you all mus' 'scuse me, d' wa'n't much upon my she'ves,

But I's done my bes' to suit you, so set down an' he'p yo'se'ves."
Tom, he 'lowed: "I don't b'lieve in 'pologisin' an' perfessin',
Let 'em tek it lak dey ketch it. Eldah Thompson, ask de blessin'."
Wish you'd seed dat colo'ed preachah cleah his th'oat an' bow his head;
One eye shet, an' one eye open,—dis is evah wud he said:
"Lawd, look down in tendah mussy on sich generous hea'ts ez dese;
Make us truly thankful, amen. Pass dat possum, ef you please!"
Well, we eat and drunk ouah po'tion, 'twell dah wasn't nothin' lef,
An' we felt jes' like new sausage, we was mos' nigh stuffed to def!
Tom, he knowed how we'd be feelin', so he had de fiddlah 'roun',
An' he made us cleah de cabin fu' to dance dat suppah down.
Jim, de fiddlah, chuned his fiddle, put some rosum on his bow,
Set a pine box on de table, mounted it an' let huh go!
He's a fiddlah, now I tell you, an' he made dat fiddle ring,
'Twell de ol'est an' de lamest had to give deir feet a fling.
Jigs, cotillions, reels an' break-downs, cordrills an' a waltz er two;
Bless yo' soul, dat music winged 'em an' dem people lak to flew.
Cripple Joe, de ole rheumatic, danced dat flo' f'om side to middle,
Th'owed away his crutch an' hopped it, what's rheumatics 'ginst a
    fiddle?
Eldah Thompson got so tickled dat he lak to los' his grace,
Had to tek bofe feet an' hol' dem so's to keep 'em in deir place.
An' de Christuns an' de sinnahs got so mixed up on dat flo',
Dat I don't see how dey'd pahted ef de trump had chanced to blow.
Well, we danced dat way an' capahed in de mos' redic'lous way,
'Twell de roostahs in de bahnyard cleahed deir th'oats an' crowed fu'
    day.
Y' ought to been dah, fu' I tell you evahthing was rich an' prime,
An' dey ain't no use in talkin', we jes had one scrumptious time!

A Note About the Author

Paul Laurence Dunbar (1872–1906) was an African American poet, novelist, and playwright. Born in Dayton, Ohio, Dunbar was the son of parents who were emancipated from slavery in Kentucky during the American Civil War. He began writing stories and poems as a young boy, eventually publishing some in a local newspaper at the age of sixteen. In 1890, Dunbar worked as a writer and editor for *The Tattler*, Dayton's first weekly newspaper for African Americans, which was a joint project undertaken with the help of Dunbar's friends Wilbur and Orville Wright. The following year, after completing school, he struggled to make ends meet with a job as an elevator operator and envisioned for himself a career as a professional writer. In 1893, he published *Oak and Ivy*, a debut collection of poetry blending traditional verse and poems written in dialect. In 1896, a positive review of his collection *Majors and Minors* from noted critic William Dean Howells established Dunbar's reputation as a rising star in American literature. Over the next decade, Dunbar wrote ten more books of poetry, four collections of short stories, four novels, a musical, and a play. In his brief career, Dunbar became a respected advocate for civil rights, participating in meetings and helping to found the American Negro Academy. His lyrics for *In Dahomey* (1903) formed the centerpiece to the first musical written and performed by African Americans on Broadway, and many of his essays and poems appeared in the nation's leading publications, including *Harper's Weekly* and the *Saturday Evening Post*. Diagnosed with tuberculosis in 1900, however, Dunbar's health steadily declined in his final years, leading to his death at the age of thirty-three while at the height of his career.

A Note from the Publisher

Spanning many genres, from non-fiction essays to literature classics to children's books and lyric poetry, Mint Edition books showcase the master works of our time in a modern new package. The text is freshly typeset, is clean and easy to read, and features a new note about the author in each volume. Many books also include exclusive new introductory material. Every book boasts a striking new cover, which makes it as appropriate for collecting as it is for gift giving. Mint Edition books are only printed when a reader orders them, so natural resources are not wasted. We're proud that our books are never manufactured in excess and exist only in the exact quantity they need to be read and enjoyed.

Discover more of your favorite classics with Bookfinity™.

- Track your reading with custom book lists.
- Get great book recommendations for your personalized Reader Type.
- Add reviews for your favorite books.
- AND MUCH MORE!

Visit **bookfinity.com** and take the fun Reader Type quiz to get started.

Enjoy our classic and modern companion pairings!